Travis I. Sivart

# Smoke & Dust

# The Traveller's Inn, Book 2

Travis I. Sivart

Travis I. Sivart

Tangled Skein

The Traveller's Inn, Book 1



ISBN: 978-1-954214-84-2

**Talk of the Tavern Publishing Group**

# Dedication

To cowboys and counterculture.

# Table of Contents

# 1. Quick Change

Jack looked around the tavern. And it was business as usual. Wanderly and Nomed sat in their usual booth, the halfling laughing uproariously and the demon-kin looking smug and full of himself. The two were an unlikely pair, one who dealt in spur-of-the-moment decisions, and the other who plotted out plans that lasted decades—and occasionally, even centuries. Jack wasn't sure why he ever handed over control of the Tavern—back when it was a floating, interdimensional submarine—to Wanderly, but it had worked out. The small man had done okay by the inn, giving it the first legs of its life.

"How's it going, gents?" Jack asked as he appeared in front of their table.

Wanderly squeaked and jumped, and Nomed stiffened—his equivalent to jumping and squeaking—and glared at Jack's sudden appearance.

"It's fine...Jack," Nomed sneered, glaring at the proprietor.

The demon liked Jack but didn't appreciate anyone who could sneak up on him, though he loved to do it to others.

"Food, okay?" Jack asked. "And plotting and planning

for the myriad of storms and stealing those jewels coming along well enough?"

Jack raised an eyebrow with a smirk, Wanderly put on an innocent countenance, and Nomed rolled his eyes.

"Yes, everything is fine." Nomed growled.

"I can whistle up a storm," Wanderly said, "and the jewels are minor magics that bring sprites and brownies to anywhere we want them. It's like a plate of cream and cornbread and will do wonders at the palace of the Serif, who said I was too short to ride his elephant!"

Nomed glared at Wanderly for spilling so much information to someone not involved in the plot.

Jack chuffed, pointing an accusing finger at the glaring man.

"You chose him as a partner and knew what he was like. So, this is on you. Why don't you two discuss it, and I'll check on the next table." Jack smiled, nodded, and moved on.

Hue Blueaxe and Grenedal Dragonblood sat in the next booth. They showed up a few decades before their world, Aetheria, tumbled into its apocalypse. Grenedal was a shadowy mix of Sherlock Holmes and Merlin, and Hue was a—literally—reborn happy-go-lucky optimist who always saw the best in others. Diametrically opposed, the two melded into a team that could get through most issues.

"Well, wishes for dark tidings," Jack purred, leaning forward and placing a hand on the table.

Grenedal had watched the man walk up, but Hue showed surprise.

"Jack!" the blue-skinned man shouted. "I didn't see you come over. Good to see you, and yes, it is dark tidings indeed. Since the Talisman haunted the skies, it has been so. Once it paused to make our sky its home, tore our world asunder, and then moved on...we've been watching and waiting. And of course, Nomed has always been a player in this game of which we speak. We need to keep a close eye on him."

"You know," Jack waved a hand in front of him, "the war has ended, the bad guys won, and the world is rebuilding. You've seen the heroes of the next age at tables in this very room. A few weeks ago, the Kid and Torrents were here. The world will be okay, and I'd suggest you find a new focus to help you move on?"

The last words were part suggestion and part question. The two men in the booth looked at one another, and when they looked back up, Jack had moved on.

The owner of the Traveller's Inn put a welcoming hand on Elementius's shoulder, nodding to the neophyte, Tilbert. Both men nodded in greeting as Jack moved on, not wanting to disrupt the discussion—or lesson—the two were engaged in.

Croaker and Kitten sat at the bar. The cyborg-warrior considered the oily drink in front of her as the rugged older man grinned and slid the glass closer to the cybernetic woman. She reached for the drink with her mechanical arm, her fingers flexing with an almost silent whir of motors and gears.

Jack considered Croaker.

The older man came from a world (the same world the danger seemed to point at currently), that was steam technology level, but had surpassed the supposed 'modern' level that Jack had been born into. Kitten came from the same world Jack had come from, just about seventy years later. Croaker had been there also, off and on (with help from Jack), and the three had gotten together for lunch more than once in that era.

It was actually all the same world—Jack thought as he glided past the two unnoticed—but he liked to think of them as different worlds. The time stream, or flow, had changed the environment so much, it was like different worlds, though it was the same planet. The atmosphere, civilization, and other factors had so many differences that it was no longer the same place, though occasionally certain things remained similar.

Jack, as a time traveller in a singular world, had seen changes that made it a different place, though he was just in a different place on the world's timeline. It fascinated him how so many people yelled and stomped their feet about time, and it being linear and concrete, when in truth time was a matter of perception. With enough change (and time) it was a different place.

Jack had seen around seventy-thousand years pass— not all at once, mind you. He jumped back and forth. And calendars tracked time according to the current society, never considering other civilizations. The man had seen decades of peace and hundreds of years of wars. He'd met gods and even was once considered a god when he tried helping folks out. It had nearly driven him mad and was one of the few times in his long life he'd grown a beard. That was a rough patch (of a few centuries) until the concept people created about him gained its own sentience.

Being a god is never a simple thing, and it can be challenging to resign from such a position.

## 2. Change Comes from Within

Cogsley leaned over the bar, pointing at a table on the far side of the room, directing Golem FloorSweeper towards the bare spot on the floor. The two were employees, of a sort. Cogsley ran the tavern portion of things for lack of a better word, and Golem was the newest employee—besides a few of the more-human wait staff, or the imps that waited in the rafters to do their duties—but was coming along nicely.

Jack hadn't considered using automatons previously, but Cogsley had kinda showed up one day when there was a need for him; and began doing things that needed done. Golem was the same, and Jack still wondered at what had created them, and who'd sent them to do the tasks they do. Perhaps it was the magic of the Inn, perhaps it was some other ability Jack had that he didn't understand, or it might just be a greater force at work.

Mogits and Manx, the newest additions to the tavern, sat at a table in front of a window. The middle-aged man—presumably a mage or wizard type—leaned towards the younger man, jabbing a finger on the tabletop to punctuate whatever he was saying. The younger man leaned back when Mogits finished and fingered the knife on his belt. Squinting and nodding slowly, the rogue agreed reluctantly to whatever Mogits had said.

Fresh additions always fascinated and worried Jack. New people meant change, and in The Traveller's Inn everything seemed random, but rarely was. The two remaining here after their adventure meant something, but Jack had yet to decipher what exactly that was.

The proprietor rubbed at his unshaven chin, contemplating what the two represented, rolling the thought of the repercussions of new folks to the regular crew around in his brain. They'd just won over impossible odds, but both had insight into a larger plot that affected the inn. But they hadn't shared those insights with Jack.

"What's going on, boss?" Darome, a gnome of some illusionary ability, asked.

Jack turned to look at the smaller man, coming back to reality.

Durg stood beside the bar, looming over his companion and friend, Darome. The ogre half-breed watched Jack, but not with curiosity or interest in his answer, but rather because his friend was interested.

This duo, like so many other pairs in the inn, were opposites. The Traveller's Inn seemed to draw pairs of people who were so unlike one another but accomplished and achieved impossible things over impossible odds that Jack never bothered to question their presence.

Cogsley slid a pint glass full of dark liquid to Jack, a thick, foamy head wobbling on the top.

Jack turned to focus on Darome, lifting a glass of thick stout to his lips, using the excuse of a drink to delay his answer. Setting the glass down after a long draw, he sighed.

"I don't know, Darome," Jack answered. "The spider queen, as the last group called her, seems to have been defeated, but I think there's more to come. I'm wondering what's next. You know what I mean?"

Darome nodded, tilting his head to consider the words. Durg also nodded in imitation of his smaller companion.

The gnome opened his mouth, then closed it, gulping back the question on his lips.

"Ask." Jack twirled his hand in a come-hither motion, using the other to raise the drink to his mouth once more.

"What's going to happen?" Darome spat out the words in a rapid patter of nervousness. "Do you think it isn't done yet? Is she going to do more? And will I get my dragon back?"

Jack barked a laugh, raising his drink to drown the response and his worry, which was apparent on his face.

"Well," Jack set the empty pint down with a clunk, and Cogsley picked it up to clean the glass, "there's change in the wind, and it blows ill. I think things will get worse before they get better. It may be best for you to go."

Darome gulped, then sputtered, "I want to stay, to help if I can. And I think Durg would agree with that."

Jack looked from the gnome to the hulking form behind him.

Durg took a beat to realize he was being included in this decision, then slowly nodded in agreement with the illusionist who'd freed him from imprisonment and slavery.

Jack knew the ogre would always agree with Darome, and the day he didn't...well, that didn't bode well for anyone.

"Oh, here it comes," Jack's face cracked with a wistful smile—an expression that could accompany a caterpillar's chrysalis fracturing to release a butterfly, or a hurricane clearing a peninsula.

"What?" Darome asked. "What's coming? Should we get under the tables?"

The windows flashed a white light from outside, then grew dark. The door chunked as the bolt crashed home, and the shutters slapped into place, a series of slams covering the openings. A sensation of dizziness spread across the room, and the regulars grabbed the edges of the table to steady themselves. They knew what was coming, having experienced it more times than they could recall. Literally.

The inn blocked the precise series of events that led up

to the changeover, and most minds couldn't handle it. Jack thought a few in the room might remember, but they knew enough to swallow the memory with an extra shot of whiskey.

The newest additions—Mogits and Manx—looked around as the spinning sensation settled across them. It was like being drunk, not a physical sensation, though it felt like it. The room spun, and if you closed your eyes, it made it worse.

The building shifted, and minor elements within the room wavered, melting into slightly different versions of themselves. Guttering oil lamps shifted, becoming a more streamlined version with metal replacing the ceramic fuel tank at the bottom. The tables became less rough and square, swapped with round and sanded tops. Along one side of the room, long plank tables shifted to green felt covered gambling tables for cards or dice.

The glass in the windows clarified, becoming clearer and more refined, and the door morphed from a solid and stout thing to something with velours and only reaching from neck to waist on most people. The outer door—a sturdier, but less so than the stout oak that had been there before—shifted to a plank closure that was pinned open by a latch.

The inn had become something like a saloon from the Old West.

Something was coming, and only Jack had a hint of what it was. He let out a sigh and turned to see what was on its way.

## 3. A Gunslinger Walks into a Bar

It always amazed Jack when the inn changed for different eras, and more so by the fact that the regulars didn't really notice a difference. Most would mentally compensate for the differences without even realizing it. It was part of the magic of the place. When it shifted, so did the perception of the inhabitants.

Again, Jack thought some people within noticed, but never said anything. Maybe that was the gift and curse of being a regular in the inn, knowing it was happening, but not being able to put your finger on what changed. The magic of the place soon wiped out the rough edges of the change, and everything seemed as it should be.

Lightning flashed outside, but not like a storm. Instead, it was as if the room was spinning really fast, with spotlights in place as points flashing past the windows and doors.

Jack gauged the reaction of the patrons within the room. Manx covered his eyes with one hand, blinking rapidly. But Mogits had risen half out of his chair, looking around to take in the effect. Wanderly looked around in wonder and awe, excited by the shifting between times and realities that he helped pioneer. Nomed leaned back on his bench seat, one hand over his eyes. Elementius and Tilbert flashed into the room, appearing at their usual table near the bar. The older scholar, Elementius, looked around with a youthful wonder, and Tilbert blinked in the flashing light as he scribbled notes. Jack thought that the two of them might one day question the movement of the inn. Croaker hunched over his drink, sipping at it carefully, and Kitten mimicked his actions. Hue and Grenedal had stopped their conversation, Hue holding his head in his hands, as the dragon-sorcerer blinked rapidly to regain his equilibrium.

And that's what this was. The Traveller's Inn was travelling, moving from one point to another. Jack, used to the visual and other effects of travelling, thought to explain it to the regulars, but doubted the wisdom of it. They might understand, or they might flip out. It was a tossup.

Jack wasn't affected like the others. To him, it was like being in a disco with a strobe going off. He'd travelled enough through his own natural abilities that this wasn't anything new or weird.

"Every time," Darome shouted, though there wasn't any extra noise to go with the event, "every time this happens, Durg gets sick!"

The ogre mix bent over and vomited noisily onto the floor. The big guy moaned, more in disappointment than any kind of suffering, and tossed a handful of peanut shells that were piled on the bar onto the moist mush mound of mouth muck.

The usual staff didn't seem to notice. The servers moved between tables with loaded trays of food, drinks, or empty dishes like nothing was happening. Some wobbled a bit on their paths of business efficiency, weaving between patrons and tables. Others stood still and waited for it to subside.

Cogsley and Golem didn't even flinch or look up as they went about their tasks. The automatons appeared to be directly connected to the inn, though Jack knew they could leave the premises, so it wasn't directly tied into their existence. Maybe just their identity?

Everything slowed and settled, and the bustle of the room picked up again.

A solid clump-shink, clump-shink, clump-shink came from outside the door. A pair of spurred boots and blue dungarees appeared under the saloon doors, but no head appeared above. The barroom doors flippy-flapped open as a short, stout man entered. His long, red whiskers hung down past his jaw, nearly to the bandana around his throat, and he glared around the saloon.

The compact man sidled to a table in a bow-legged swagger, his elbows crooked over the twin revolvers hanging low on his hips.

"Is this guy going to a showdown or what?" Darome said in a stage whisper that the entire room could hear.

"Draw!" Wanderly shouted.

The man's hands, lightning quick, blurred and twin barrels pointed directly at Wanderly.

Nomed was up on his feet in a flash, placing himself between the halfling and the stranger, a huge caliber hand cannon pointed at the stranger.

"Whoa there, gentlemen," Jack stepped between the metal tubes of death, wiping his hands on the newly appeared white apron hanging on his waist, "there's no need for all that now. It was just a jest meant to lighten the mood."

"Oh, that sort of thing don't lighten a mood," the stranger said, dropping his pistols back into their holsters. "That sort of thing gets you shot, ya rattle brained idjit!"

He fired the last comment across the room, directed towards Wanderly. The halfling didn't seem to get hit hard by it, grinning and winking.

"Wouldn't be the first time my mouth got me into trouble," Wanderly giggled. "Others like to point out that for a small guy, I have a big mouth."

"Well, they ain't wrong," the newcomer growled, flopping onto a chair. "Barkeep, bring me a sarsaparilla!"

The hubbub and ambient noise of the inn picked up

again as the servers delivered drinks and food, and the regulars settled into their usual activities.

The stranger saw Cogsley nod and turn away, focusing on the array of taps on the back wall connected to various kegs and pipes that rose to the ceiling. Polished copper and brass tubes wound and twisted behind the bar, some sweating with their cooler temperatures, and others showing a wisp of steam wafting from them in their heat.

Jack pushed from the bar, leaving Darome and Durg behind, as he walked across the room towards the newest addition to the Inn. His feet crossed as he walked, not quite stumbling, but not walking a straight line.

Arriving at the table, Jack leaned on it with one hand and smiled down at the short man.

"Hey there," Jack said, not quite sure what else to say.

"Not interested," the stranger waved a hand at Jack.

"Okay then," Jack sighed, "Not what I meant, but I'll go ahead and...um, go away."

## 4. A Spoonful of Sugar

The inn was desolate, if you didn't bother counting the automations and the four lingering souls who were drinking way past the hours that common sense dictated when you should have a drink and an attitude.

Cogsley leaned on the bar, his glass dome head cradled in a white gloved hand, his other hand idly wiping at the countertop that already shone with a luster that came from being abused for countless hours of polishing cloths. The wires inside his globule of a noggin flickered, as his ideas shifted, and showed the wandering thoughts he was having.

Golem FloorSweeper sighed, pushing their massive broom across an already cleaned floor, mounds of sawdust curling onto itself in front of the clay creature as they swept through the room. Imps sighed a moment later, dropping from the rafters to spread more sawdust from their satchels to re-cover the floor with the absorbent shavings that protected the hardwood from drinks, blood, and other bodily fluids.

Two strangers sat at two different tables, glaring at one another, but in a way that told everyone else that they weren't strangers to one another.

"Calamity Sam," the man with the long, bushy,

hanging red moustache growled, staring at the woman at the next table.

"Tawny Tiffene," the woman sneered, sliding a dark brown braid of hair away from her brown eyes, "and I remember you, Sam, and I don't rightly like your attitude."

Croaker nudged the woman with the metal arm beside him, snickering and pointing at the two. She looked at him and shrugged in indifference and confusion. The older man made a series of bodily motions—something like interpretive dance while seated on a bar stool—and waited for her bewildered look to shift to understanding.

It didn't.

"Ooooh, I don't like your face, Tawny Tiffene," Calamity Sam retorted, "will Airhorn Bobborn and Plains Jane be here soon, or do I have to stare at your face long enough to make me sick?"

"That doesn't even make a lick of sense, you doe-eyed, cross-eyed, sack-licking, sad-sack of a man." Tiffene smiled triumphantly at what she felt was a supreme comeback to the short man's question.

The doors slammed open, framing a woman in the sunrise's dawning light.

"Hey bitches, what's up?" a brazen feminine voice asked.

All heads—human, cyborg, and automaton alike—turned to look at the door.

Silhouetted in the dual-flippy saloon doors that led from the porch to the interior of the inn, Plains Jane's stout, thick form—fists on hips—stood framed in the portal. She stomped forward, her spurs chinging with every step she took, then she stopped. Her grimace of seriousness spread to a smile of delight and amusement, and her arms flung wide.

"Calamity Sam and Tawny Tiffene, if it ain't you two tumbleweeds dancing the scrub tango again, I'll be my uncle's monkey!"

"I don't think you quite got that turn of phrase correct,

Jane," Tiffene mumbled, her brow crinkling as her attention was drawn from her frenemy.

"Awww," Sam's voice ripped through the air like a sheet of paper being torn, "what the dang-burned hells are you talking about, you addled-brained woman?"

"My uncle had a monkey, and boy! Didn't that little guy love to dance? He did it straight up until the day he died, which came the same day he attacked a fat man who wouldn't give him a cookie. He beat that man black and blue, hugging the engorged dome of his head, snatching at the chocolate wafers with the white sugary middle, and then took a ham-fist to his ribs, and three slugs afterwards. I saw it all and learned one thing...never try to take a cookie from a fat man who's pissed."

All six of the people inside the Traveller's Inn stared at Plains Jane, unsure what response would be appropriate to that particular story.

"Welcome," Cogsley raised his head and greeted the woman, "and how may I be of service? Food, whores, fine drinks, or just a room? What would be your personal preference?"

"Well," Jane straightened up and smiled, "don't all those things all sound delightful? But the truth is, I just want these two rapscallions to behave, and Airhorn Bobborn to show up so we can get on with this show of contingencies!"

"Very good, madam, may I offer to take your...duster?" Cogsley asked, drawling the words with his overly proper accent.

"Naw, but you can go out and take care of my horse, Bullseye, if'n you don't mind. He's friendly, worse he's gonna do is love you to death. Unless he hears a gun, then he gets downright mean. So, if'n you don't go shooting at him, you should be just fine!"

"Of course," Cogsley nodded, "Golem, please go take care of Mz. Jane's beast of burden. I believe we still have spots available in the garage. And by garage, I meant stable."

"Yep," the automaton almost moaned the word, "I'd

love to go pet the horsey. Nothing more exciting than rubbing down a sweaty beast. It's in my top four-hundred things to do."

Jane intercepted Golem, put a hand on his shoulder and stopped him.

"Thank you for taking care of Bullseye, and here's something that might help you out." She held out a fist above his hand.

The clay construct slowly raised their hand, turned it, and opened it. A few sugar cubes and some coins clinked against Golem's hardened, reddish palm. They closed their hand around the items as Jane rubbed their shoulder and smiled at them.

The automaton tilted their head, their expressionless face unmoving, but their mild bewilderment showing through their body language.

"The coins are for you," Jane explained, still smiling, "maybe buy yourself a neckerchief, or a nice hat. Hats make the outfit, you know? And the sugar cubes are for Bullseye, he just melts for them. But you could try one too, if'n you really wanna. I won't mind, though Bullseye might if'n you don't give him one first."

# 5. Pointing Fingers

The hulking figure just nodded, then slowly turned back to the door, and schlepped outside into the early morning light. "Okay, you two!" Jane turned towards Sam and Tiffene, shifted her stance to shoulder width, planted her fists on her hips, and looked down at the two. "You know you can't be fighting all the time. So, let's all get to the same table and talk this thing out."

The woman looked back and forth between the two, watching Sam's dour glower, and Tiffene's haughty disdain.

"Look, even the guy at the bar and the woman next to him are watching the spectacle you're creating. I swear, they're about to order popcorn and shout things like you were two unprofessional actors on a stage!" Jane said.

"Okay then, Calamity Sam, you come on over to Tawny Tiffene's table," Plains Jane pointed to match her words, then held up a hand as Sam opened his mouth to protest. "Don't say a word! You got a window seat, which is the first-place people shoot someone. She's got something in the middle of the room, but it's near the fireplace, so it'll be warmer, and it's autumn, season of chills and sniffles, and it'll do us good. Besides, we need to learn to watch each other's backs, unlike when we had that issue up in Gully Gulch last year."

Both Tiffene and Sam raised a hand to point at the other, but Jane cut them off with a crisp word.

"Nuh uh, you ain't gonna point fingers," she growled, "we're just gonna move on. So, Sam, get yer ass over here. Don't make me use my lasso, you lug."

The short man sighed and stood, his chair flying backwards. He picked up his foaming glass mug of beer and stalked towards Tiffene's table.

Jane looked the short man over. He hadn't changed much, and that was to be expected when traveling light and moving from territory to territory in the frontier lands. He wore his usual blue dungarees, red shirt, and yellow kerchief. The wide brim of his hat was folded up, showing a broad forehead and bushy eyebrows. His protuberant nose shadowed his bushy red moustache that hung down well past his chin.

Tawny Tiffany, on the other hand, was his stylistic opposite, and dressed in a pale turquoise dress. Hell, it could almost be called a gown, the diaphanous over-dress muting the colors of the underdress. A thick brown braid draped over her shoulder, a golden brooch clipped to the end to stop any hairs from escaping and tarnishing her appearance. The woman's pert nose, as always, tilted upward in a pose of contempt and superiority.

Jane compared her own pale green gingham shirt, mustard-yellow dungarees, and leather chaps to the outfits of the others. They were like three peas in a pod, if peas were polar opposites, and the world had three poles. Four, if you counted Airhorn Bobborn. He was another story altogether.

Jane looked back and forth between the two, her plain brown ponytail—tied back with a rawhide strap—bouncing across her shoulders.

Smiling, she turned to Tiffene.

"So, what have you been up to?" Jane asked. "Getting any better with those ice powers?"

"Hush," Tiffene hunched and looked left and right. "Someone might hear you. And you know they'll lynch someone for being able to do these things. It's not as bad as the witch hunts a hundred years ago, but it isn't much better. Magic is frowned upon with the dampening of religion and the uptick of the science arts, though religion never actually embraced it unless you called it a miracle instead of the other options."

The three leaned in, the effort of re-connecting and comparing stories of events since they'd last seen each other rolling across the cracked tabletop. They talked for hours, alternately arguing and commiserating over life's hardships and challenges they had dealt with since they'd last been in the same room.

The lunch crowd rolled in, laborers and dayworkers creeping in like they'd never been here before, which they hadn't. The imps darted from the rafters above—disguised as small zeppelins for the current crowd of patrons—and dusted the floor with sawdust to soak up the spills. Men and women in long white aprons rushed throughout the room, delivering steins and tankards alongside plates of steaming vittles and helpings of biscuits. Everything came with biscuits, which were either rock hard or steaming fresh, depending on the attitude of the patron.

The Traveller's Inn was a travelling business, as in it appeared and disappeared from one location to the next. Fun fact, the locals never noticed that it hadn't been there the whole time, or that it suddenly disappeared when either of the aforementioned events happened.

The saloon doors flippy-flopped open. An immense man in a stark white suit, with yellow shoes, and a bright red bowler hat entered. It was nearly high-noon—an infamous time for gunslingers and clock makers—and he blinked into the dim interior of the saloon doors that now were the common entry way of The Traveller's Inn.

"Airhorn!" Calamity Sam hollered, waving a hand over his head, a look close to relief on his face.

Airhorn Bobborn, slouched towards the sound, blinking into the middle distance.

"I say, I say boy, how you doing?" The man in the pristine alabaster suit shouted. "You look as fit as a cricket in a haystack, boy!"

"Is that really a thing?" Tiffene muttered.

"Bobborn!" Jane yelled, leaping from her ladder-back chair and running across the saloon.

She threw herself through the air and the older southern man caught her in a two-handed grip. He spun her in a circle and set her down, holding her at arm's length.

"Girlie," Bobborn said, "if'n you ain't a sight for sore eyes! How's that filly of yours, Bullseye?"

"Aw, geez," Jane ran a toe along the sawdust, "she's just peachy, full of vim and vigor, and ready to throw herself towards whatever crosses us. Thanks for inquiring. She'll be downright giddy that you asked after her."

Turning toward the table, Airhorn Bobborn almost tripped over Calamity Sam. The taller man, head-and-shoulders above Sam, stumbled to a stop before tripping over the shorter man.

## 6. Sit a Spell

"Ooooh, you're a welcome attraction, um, I meant distraction…in this dusty, one-horse town," Sam intoned, holding a hand towards Bobborn. "The locals are plumb loco, if you catch my drift. Stubborn as a mule, and twice as thick!"

"Sam, if'n anyone knows about stubborn, it's you, my diminutive friend." Bobborn shook the man's hand and gestured towards the table with his free hand. "Now, I'd love to sit a spell, trade tales, and get a heapin' plate of something hot to shovel in."

The three moved to the table and settled into chairs. Bobborn waved to a man in a white apron with a chiseled chin and a scruffy beard that looked like it wished for better days.

"A plate of stew," Airhorn's voice was louder than needed, "and some of those there biscuits I've been seeing floating around."

The four gathered around the table, leaning in to scoop their food into their faces, wet slurping noises settling over the conversation. The meal was simple and common, but the brown gravy that covered almost everything was thick, rich, and flavored enough to make a camel give up drinking.

Chunks of greasy mutton swam in the dark brown liquid, carrots, and peas, making appearances on the surface before diving back under. Chunks of potatoes were like small off-white islands in the sea of stew until scooped up on a spoon and torn from their native environment. Servers brought tall glass mugs to the table, foaming heads and deep-amber liquid making mouths water for a whole different reason.

You need to understand, before mass-marketing was a thing, people would make food and drink for the love of it and be rewarded in fame or infamy rather than dollars. As time progressed, the tradeoff was made, and quality suffered for the all-mighty dollar. The plates of stew and the house beer had come from an era before sellouts.

The table was far from silent, but the only time you heard a voice was under the guise of a small grunt of pleasure, or a moan of a yummy noise. Beers kept coming, and biscuits flowed like a floury avalanche of buttered arterial destruction.

Sam and Bobborn got into a bit of a competition with the beers, seeing who could consume more than the other. Jane silently competed, knowing she could out-drink either of the men, as she'd done more than once on their last outing together. She wasn't allowed to compete anymore, not because they wouldn't let her, but because she felt it was too easy to win.

The two men squinted like it was still high noon—when Bobborn had entered the inn—and were about to draw their holstered steel, like Sam did when he'd entered the inn. They stared at one another, spoons in one hand, ready to draw a slurp of stew to their mouths, and a mug handle in the other, ready to deliver liquid refreshment to their lips to wash down a dry bite, or an overloaded mouthful.

Sam was the clear winner, despite his size. Bobborn rocked and blinked in his seat, but the smaller man sat firm and erect in his, smiling at his larger dining companion.

They leaned back after a spell. Pushing away tin pie pans, wiped clean with a biscuit, each person showing appreciation for the meal in their own individual way. Tiffene leaned back, smiled, and sighed. Bobborn rubbed his rounded belly and chuckled to himself. Sam stretched his arms far above his head, leaning back on two legs of his chair, groaning in pleasure from the meal. Plains Jane slapped her gut, belched loudly, and let out a whoop of delight, looking around at the table with bright eyes and a wide smile.

"So," Airhorn Bobborn broke the silence, "whatta we got?"

"Scarecrows," Plains Jane grinned, "they're everywhere. It seems that Crow Row, a little out of the way collection of farmers, has had a bunch of scarecrows popping up."

"That's stupid," Calamity Sam growled. "Farmers put up scarecrows all the time."

"Yes, that's true." Tawny Tiffene nodded. "Why would we care about a bunch of scarecrows?"

"Because," Jane leaned in, and the others did the same, "these particular farmers didn't put them up. These scarecrows appear overnight, lining the outer perimeter of the cornfields. And people disappear without a trace as the number of scarecrows grow."

The other three stared at the horse woman, their brows wrinkling in confusion.

"There's a reward to find out why these things are appearing." Jane muttered, and the other three let out a collective sound of understanding and interest. "And here's the weirdest part...they're wearing the clothes of the missing townsfolk."

The others leaned back, their brows raising in interest.

"Good times, right?" a fresh voice cut through their private conversation.

All four jerked back and upright to look at the newcomer standing next to their table.

The man was dressed in a brown duster and dungarees, and a white shirt without the top two buttons done. He was plain, but in the way that didn't stand out as common.

"I'm Jack, the proprietor of this establishment," the man smiled, "and I couldn't help but overhear that you're considering going out to Crow Row to investigate the recent disturbance of the town."

"I say, I say, why should we care who you are, and why should we want you shoving your nose into our business?" Bobborn blurted.

Sam nodded his agreement, and Tiffene turned to glare across the table at the man's rudeness.

"Why, boys," Jane smiled and waved a hand at Jack, "this here is the man who will be supplying the reward when we get back. So we should at least keep a civil tongue in our heads when talking with him."

Airhorn Bobborn stood, his chair sliding backwards and falling over with a clatter. The room fell silent. He held a whiskey in one hand and put his other on the table as he wobbled on his feet. He blinked into the air in front of him, then turned to look towards where he'd last heard Jack's voice.

# 7. Snipes and Wumpus

"Sir," Bobborn intoned, his booming voice echoing through the eerie hollow quiet of the busy tavern, "I offer my most sincere apologies for my boisterous and bombastic bluster. It was rude and uncalled for, and I hope you might find it in your heart to forgive someone who spoke without thinking. My mouth, I say, I say, my mouth got the best of my brain, and beat it to a broken thing that never had a chance of competing."

Jack stared, his head cocked and his eyebrows coming together. He cleared his throat, nodded, and smiled.

"Of course," the proprietor cleared his throat, obviously off balance from the exchange, "I-I think we can move on, and talk about money, glory, or whatever you people think needs to happen."

"You people?" Tiffene smiled a sardonic grin, her white teeth contrasting with her mocha skin, her beauty shining through. She laughed as Jack's face showed his backpedaling. "I'm messing with you, Jack. Calm down and go on."

"Okay..." he drew the word out, his eyes darting around the table, his discomfort apparent, "well, the town of Crow Row was once a farming community, and then the train came through, laying tracks and bringing the commerce of the east to the west. But it was just about a little more than a year ago, things went wonky. Thirteen widows showed up, bought a ranch outside of town, and began employing every roustabout, farmhand, and drunk they could find to plant corn. They did offer a few other crops, but nothing to match the corn..."

"Ooooh," Calamity Sam interrupted, "get to the dang-burned point, before you bore us to dozing in our breeches."

"Okay, right, okay," Jack muttered, still off balance, "things changed. As their crops grew, they needed fewer and fewer farm hands, but more and more scarecrows to keep watch over the fields. People started disappearing, and the population of people of stakes grew. Hundreds of scarecrows popped up. And anyone who came around looking for them usually didn't come back."

"Snipes and Wumpus?" Jane asked, and all heads turned to look at her. "What I'm trying to ask is, are we looking for something that is nothing short of rumor, myth, and legend?"

"Yeah," Jack nodded slowly, "something like that. And it's not something you can just ask a local without risking a lynching."

"Pfft," Tiffene scoffed, "you're asking a lot from this group, then. We're not known for subtlety and finesse."

Plains Jane laughed, a sound like a braying mule.

"What?" Bobborn demanded. "We aren't a bull in a shop of fine dishes...I believe they call it Shinnae, after the Aeifain artists that make the best dishes, layered with ceramics from centuries of skill."

They all stopped talking, turning to look at the big man from the southern part of North Mirron.

Bobborn had his uses, but no one would actually call him a friend. From his slouched, casual posture, to his beak of a nose, and added onto his preening strut and his bold, outspoken ways, Airhorn wasn't the easiest person to like.

Add in his proclivity to verbally bully folks to get one over on them, and even his close acquaintances watched him carefully before trusting what he said.

"I think he's right," Jack nodded. "Fine, Shinnae is the correct term."

"So," Tiffene breathed, "when do we leave?"

"I don't see the point of waiting around," Sam growled, and jammed two fingers of chewing tobacco between his lip and gum.

"Indeed," Bobborn shouted, "right after one more round of drinks, I think we'll be ready to head to the hills. Barkeep! Set up another round for me and my friends and bring our horses around when we're done."

Jack moved away as Golem moved in, another tray of drinks in hand. The construct dropped off the beverages and shuffled away, muttering about the futility of drinking away eternal pain.

"Look," Tiffene sat up straight, "we've worked together before, and we all know this could quickly go to shit. I need you all to remember that I am an elementalist..."

"Using the term loosely," Sam muttered.

"An elementalist," Tiffene repeated through gritted teeth while glaring at the moustachioed man, "and we can't talk about that in public. Again. Do we all understand that?"

Jane nodded but winked at the two men.

"I think, I daresay, we all learned our lesson about that last time," Bobborn said, and the others laughed with the memory.

Bobborn and Sam raised their whiskey glasses and clinked them together.

"What do you bring to the table, Jane?" Tiffene asked. "I mean, really, is riding a horse and being good with a rope something that gets you an equal share?" The ice queen held up a hand to forestall anyone from answering. "Think about it for just a moment," Tiffene continued. "Sam is a sharpshooter with his pistols. Bobborn could talk his way out of an outhouse hole, with a mouthful of shit, and finger in the other man's ass and come out smelling nicer than a dozen roses…"

"That sounds like a good night out to me," Sam muttered, earning another glare from Tiffene.

"Okay now, Tiffene." Jane raised her voice to get the table's attention. "No, you had your say. Now, it's my turn. I'll tell you what I bring to the table, and when I'm done, I think we'll all agree I'm utterly needed for this outing to be a success."

Plains Jane stood up, and leaned on the table, both palms flat on the wooden top.

"I keep this group together." Jane said, plainly. "Sam and Bobborn would drink or fight if left to their own devices, and it may be with townsfolk, or with each other, ya just never know!" The two men traded glances and smiles, then shrugged and nodded their agreement.

"I find the real clues and sniff out the trail." Jane stated this as a simple truth. "Without me, this group would flounder and wander. I keep ya'll on the straight and narrow."

"You make it sound like you're the leader," Tiffene snorted, "when we all know that I'm the one in charge of this…"

The wizardess never finished her thought, as the table erupted into arguing.

## 8. Don't Let the Door Hit Ya

Jack watched the four people known as Calamity Sam, Bobborn Airhorn, Plains Jane, and Tawny Tiffene leave the tavern. He watched Plains Jane vault into her saddle as Bobborn and Tiffene climbed into theirs.

"Dagnabbit, ya beast," Sam yelled, "stay still!"

Calamity Sam wrestled with the bridle of his horse, trying to get the animal under control. The small man managed to get one foot into a stirrup, bouncing forward as his horse sidestepped in a small circle, then swung a leg across the saddle.

"Yah, mule!" Sam shouted, slapping his boot heels against the mount's sides. "Giddyap, ya varmint. Aww, come on!"

The other three trotted away, small clouds of dust puffing into the air under the hoof-falls of their mounts, looking over their shoulders towards Sam.

"Think they'll survive?" Croaker Norge asked from over Jack's shoulder, making the man jump.

"We've seen worse," Jack said.

"Have we really, though?" Croaker asked.

"You're lucky I didn't ask you to go," Jack took a deep breath to settle his nerves. "You know the era, and the territory. You grew up here on North Mirron and have travelled most of it from the Empire to the Dasism Territories out west. You've experienced more than most people will ever realize is even out there."

"Naw, this is more of the arena of expertise of Spenser and Trudy Tridington." The old man said, cradling his mug of brew. "They know about the weird and crazy shit like this. Tentacle-faced critters from the Old Gods. But is this that? Or is it something new?"

"I don't think it's either," Jack sighed. "I think it's related to the crap we saw with Mogits and that shadowy thief kid. What was his name? Began with an 'M'?"

"Manx?" Croaker suggested.

"Yeah, that's the one." Jack nodded. "I think that ethereal spider queen is still trying to get her appendages into the tavern. She wants something from us."

"What do you think that is?" Croaker asked.

"Not sure." Jack shrugged. "Could be the energy source of what powers the Inn, or it could be as simple as wanting to destroy a natural competitor in her ecosystem."

"Ever think she could want the inn so she can move about time and space, unburdened?" Croaker picked up his mug and took a deep drink.

"Durg think she want Jack," the ogre at the end of the bar said.

All eyes turned to the behemoth.

Darome swallowed with an audible gulp, picked up a shot of whiskey that belonged to Croaker, and threw it back. The grizzled old detective winced as the little man gasped at the strength of the drink. "You don't fool around, do you?" Darome rasped.

"Not with booze, and not with women," Croaker said, slapping the smaller man on the shoulder.

"Jack?" Darome squeaked.

Jack turned to look at the gnome and realized the entire public room was watching him with concerned looks.

"Could she be coming for you?" Darome asked.

"Yeah," Jack sighed with a nod. "She could be. I've made a lot of enemies in my lifetime. My many lifetimes."

"You've made a lot of friends, too." Grenedal said from across the bar.

"And we've got your back," Nomed added grimly. "No one takes what's ours. And Jack, you belong to us. And we'll make that very clear to anyone coming for you. Don't doubt that for a second."

"Yeah!" Wanderly added helpfully.

"Thanks everyone," Jack smiled, but the confidence and bravado of his expression fell short of being convincing. "I'm just saying we should be prepared for whatever happens."

"Sir?" a droning voice intoned from behind the bar. "Do you think we should fire up the engines and make ourselves scarce?"

"I don't think it would help, Cogsley," Jack sighed again, "I think she's set her sights on us, and nothing more than removing her as a threat will help make the Traveller's Inn free and not an object of conquest."

"You know," a high-pitched voice from a corner booth chimed in, "I did set up the phlogiston engines to whip us away to somewhere else when I made them, and it might give us some distance from her reach."

"Wanderly," the deep baritone of Baron Von Nomed said, "I think Jack knows that, and he even most likely considered that. I believe he has a larger plot in mind when he keeps sending out these bands of nare-do-wells, miscreants, and losers to fight our battles. Though I do think a more direct and frontal assault on an ethereal and abysmal enemy may be the better plan."

Jack turned back to the room. All the regulars watched him, their expressions expectant. He looked across the gathering.

Golem swept the floor, the automaton's eyes watching him from the shadows of their thick brow. Cogsley stood behind the bar, wiping the polished surface with a clean white cloth. Croaker took a step backwards towards his drinking buddy, Kitten—the female cyborg with the mechanical arm—and smiled sheepishly. Wanderly, the halfling, and Nomed, the demon half-breed, sat in their customary booth, and a few others waited expectantly for his reassuring words.

"Look," Jack started, then hesitated, "we can charge in, but she expects that. Cutting off the arms doesn't work, let's find the head. Lashing out blindly before we know what she's really doing will just let her plot go beyond what we already know. The Queen wants that. She desires the energy that powers our inter-dimensional home. This place puts out lots of threads of power, right?"

The group nodded, only knowing select parts of the entire story.

"We need to see the bigger game," Jack continued. "Think of this as a chess match. We have pawns, rooks, knights, bishops, and other pieces."

"Like kings and queens?" Wanderly asked nervously, his voice shrill.

Jack shuddered, unused to the smaller man sounding anything less than confident.

"Yeah, kings and queens," Jack breathed, "but I just don't know if those pieces are us or someone else. That's the problem with projecting. You never know which piece you are, or if you're even the player."

## 9. On The Road Again

Tawny Tiffene stretched in her saddle, looking at the others in the small group. Her roan mare snorted and danced sideways on the dusty trail leading to the small town of Crow Row.

The elementalist looked at her companions, judging their worth and ability. Airhorn Bobborn was their diplomat, but not in the traditional sense. He was a bull in a Shinnae shop, breaking as many connections as he made, but in this area, people responded well to that kind of personality. Though being drunk most of the time could be a good thing or a bad thing. The man was a lummox, but his grating ways often made others stop and listen before doing anything else.

Calamity Sam was an expert with his dual pistols, but his temper created more issues than his twin barrels usually fixed. He was worse than a child with a stick standing under a beehive. Yelling was his regular form of communication, and this cowed some folks, but made the hackles of others rise.

Plains Jane was another story altogether. She was the spirit of the group. Jane was an optimist, always expecting things to go their way, even when everything was falling apart. She was a master of the horse, able to perform feats and tricks that surpassed any show or trick riding Tiffene had seen. The woman could also do things with a lariat that would put a gymnast spider to shame.

Tiffene was unsure of her own worth. She had some ability with elemental magic, a little air, and a little water. Mostly, she excelled at combining the two into ice and everything that could be drawn from that bailiwick. The others were in awe of her powers, but she knew the limitations and almost feared their confidence in her.

But she also knew the benefits of perception, marketing, and branding. You can be a self-made person, but if you can convince others of what you want them to see you as, then they can help you become that. It followed the whole 'fake it until you make it' philosophy, but with the added impetus of them telling you what you want to be because you told them.

The other three were sweating, rivulets of moisture running down their faces, and their armpits stained with perspiration. Tiffene, however, was as cool as a fine autumn day due to her magics. Though it was autumn, the arid climate didn't show it. The night would drop to cooler temperatures, cold even, and perhaps a frost by morning if there was enough humidity.

The town of Crow Row came into sight, drawing Tiffene's attention from her thoughts. An inverted "L" shaped post jutted over the hard-packed dirt road, a creaking sign on rusted chains and a dilapidated board proclaiming the name of the weathered buildings ahead.

The main thoroughfare bustled, as much as with tumbleweeds and stray dogs as merchants and townsfolk. Ruts ran down the middle of the street, worn into the road from the rainy season, and solidified in the dry months. The town hall, a three-story affair of brick and wood, sat at the end of the thoroughfare. The standard businesses lined the main street; a blacksmith, saloon and gambling hall, hotel and bathhouse, bank and assayer's office, sheriff, mercantile and general store, barber and surgeon, stable, and a telegraph office which also offered the latest in communication...a Lightbox house, which operated on Baron Von Nomed's Wireless Electric Delivery Sky System, better known as WEDSS. That meant that some folks may even have a Personal Telegraph Device (or PTD) which often was a leather bracer with a brass telegraph instrument atop it.

A half-kilometer outside of town was an airship tower, waiting to house zeppelins or low or high airships, such as the Regency Talon 320 Airship, a Raython Windrider 120, or even one of the latest in hovercraft, the Hyperion Lightning, one of the rare high airships. At the moment, though, the tower was deserted and looked to be in ill repair.

Every building down Main Street, and the adjoining streets, looked to be in equal states of disrepair. Wagons trundled down the road, dust trailing behind them, with men in overalls and women in gingham dresses crossing behind them.

The four moseyed into the collection of buildings that made up the town. Sam grumbled about a burr in his boot and spat a wad of brown spittle into the dirt. Bobborn took a swig from his flask and scratched his belly, but Jane was the outlier. She stood in her stirrups, looking around excitedly.

"Well, Bullseye," she stroked her horse's neck, "this looks like a fine place. Maybe get you some oats, or pick me up an extra shirt! Maybe something with mother-of-pearl buttons in a fine check pattern? Whatdya think?"

The horse snorted and walked forward; her head held high as the animal surveyed the area.

"Should we start at the saloon, and then check the hotel for rooms, or the other way around?" Tiffene asked as she brushed dust off her clothes.

"I say, I say," Bobborn Airhorn's voice made heads turn to look at the group, "I think that a stop at the saloon is the best way to get some information—not to mention a quick wetting of the whistle—and the best way to go."

Everyone grunted or nodded their agreement, knowing that arguing with the man would do no good.

The locals—noticing the group because of the loud man's voice—moved to the side of the street and watched the small procession. It was like being their own personal parade, though the small gathering didn't cheer at their passing. Eyes either glared at them or turned down and away when they looked at the townsfolk.

The group reined in at the saloon, the sign hanging over the rail to tie off horses proclaiming it to be 'Adam's Saloon'. They slid from their mounts, Jane running her leather-gloved hand along Bullseye's neck and pushing a quartered apple towards the animal's expectant and quivering lips. Bobborn moaned, stretching and groaning as he dismounted.

Sam yelled, "Woah, mule, woah! I said, woah!"

The animal slowed, then stopped, and the red-bearded man fell off the horse.

"You always have to make an entrance, dontcha, boy?" Bobborn said to the prone man.

## 10. Beer & Brats

The boom of a shotgun blast caused everyone to stop in their tracks. The townsfolk in the street froze, except for a few who nervously shuffled their feet or juggled their bundles to keep them in their hands. A baby wailed in the crowd and a dog barked repeatedly from somewhere behind the buildings.

"Of course," Tiffene muttered, looking around, "which one of you did something stupid?"

Calamity Sam was on his feet, his hands hovering just above his twin pistols. The short man squinted towards the sound of gunfire, his bushy eyebrows bristling.

Bobborn Airhorn smiled and pulled out a flask, untwisting the cap and slugging back a drink. Barely a dribble came out. The big man glared at the flask like it had betrayed him.

Plains Jane petted Bullseye with the hand holding the reins, and her other hand settled onto the butt of her sidearm. She slid closer to her shotgun in its harness beside her saddle.

A bowlegged man trundled forward, crazy white hair writhing in the wind, and squinted at the group of newcomers.

"Who're you now?" he drawled.

"We're just…" Tiffene began, only to be cut off by Sam.

"We're you're great Aunt Tilly's university barber shop quartet," Sam growled, "and we're here to woo her until she picks her favorite to sleep with tonight."

"My Aunt Tilly is a saint!" The man exclaimed. "And none of you look old enough to have gone to uni with her!"

"Pay no mind to that miscreant," Tiffene said, raising her voice to be heard. "He's a drunkard and an imbecile. We've come to the quaint village of Crow Row…"

A huge hand pushed Tawny Tiffene to one side, and Bobborn stumbled in front of her.

"I say, I say, boy," Bobborn bellowed, "don't pay no mind to the little lady, she's just flustered."

"He's right," Sam shouted, shoving up beside his towering companion, "and I'm no drunkard. Bobborn's the drunkard! I'm the mean-spirited, ornery, grouchy fellow who hates everyone!"

"He ain't wrong," Bobborn grinned, then hiccupped.

Plains Jane facepalmed as Tiffene fumed, her fists clenched at her sides.

"As I was saying, I say, as I was saying," Bobborn went on, "you know how the womenfolk get all excited, not like us menfolk, we just get angry or loud…"

The wild-haired man stepped in front of the group and shoved the double barrels of his rifle under Bobborn's chin. The big man verbally stumbled to a halt and gulped.

"You better start talking, and now, or else Ol' Bessy here is gonna get mighty testy, and my finger's gonna get mighty twitchy." The older man growled.

"Chrysler?" Plains Jane leaned around Bullseye.

"Jane?" The older man leaned forward. "Is that you, girl?"

"It's me, you old codger!" The horsewoman squealed, running forward to embrace the man.

Chrysler dropped the gun from Bobborn's chin and

awkwardly hugged Jane with one arm.

"Well," the man said, "why didn't you say so?" He turned to the crowd, his arm still around Jane's waist. "Do you know who this is?" he asked.

The crowd murmured, many shaking their heads.

"This is the woman who single-handedly tracked down and rounded up the rustlers who stole two-hundred head of cattle from me a few years ago. She's a sharp shooter with a mouth and mind to match!"

The crowd murmured again, this time appreciatively.

"Aw, shucks!" Jane said, trailing a toe in the dirt street. "I didn't do nuthin nobody else wouldn't have done."

"Well, come on, girl!" Chrysler said, "I think I still owe you that drink!"

Sam and Bobborn slapped their mouths shut, breaking into grins when they heard mention of a drink, and moved to follow.

"Oh, no you don't!" Tiffene huffed, grabbing both men by an ear, causing them both to squeal. "You two are going to stable the horses, rub them down, and stow our gear before you can have a drink. And you will wash your face and hands before sitting at a table with me, and I don't mean in the horse trough!"

"But I didn't…" Sam began.

"I don't see how…" Bobborn said.

"Shut it!" Tiffene snapped. "And if either of you ever interrupt me like that again, you're going to wake as a frozen popsicle in your sleeping roll the next morning!"

"You're mayor and sheriff?" Jane asked, gaping at Chrysler.

"Well, there's been a shortage of people to do all the jobs," Chrysler explained, blushing, "ever since everyone started going missing."

The four friends sat around a table in Adam's Saloon,

joined by Chrysler. Everyone passing smiled at the man, though some patted him sympathetically on the shoulder.

The place was run by Samuel Adams's and his wife, Stella. The man had a pageboy haircut of brown hair and smiled a lot. A brown leather vest with brass buttons accented his pristine white shirt, and he regularly raised his metal tankard of his own brew to patrons. Stella, not to be outdone, wore a low-cut white blouse that accented her cleavage, a deep blue skirt, and a leather corset.

Bud, a young boy, ran around taking drink orders, trailed by his dog, Spuds Growler. The dog was a white, thick-bodied terrier with a black ring around one eye. It was wide of shoulder and had dark eyes that glared at the strangers, but then padded up to a regular, tail wagging and tongue lolling out to one side.

The saloon was a wood and brass affair, a large mirror behind the bar. A dozen unlabeled bottles lined the shelf, and glasses frosted with age and scouring hung from hooks and hanging racks, depending on if they were mugs or stemware.

"Something weird has been going on though," Chrysler said, "I'll tell you that. You saw the rows of scarecrows in the fields outside of town, two deep now!"

"Yeah," Bobborn said, "creepy. But at least the beer is excellent here."

"I think it's those witches!" A woman stood over them, warty nose and bulbous chin jutting over them.

## 11. Hags & Handshakes

The woman glared down at the table, her one good eye shifting from person to person. She was barely thirty years old, but every patron in the saloon looked at her with fear or awe. Her clothes were ratty rags, accented by glittering rings and a silver and ruby necklace.

She flared her skirt with bony hands and grinned, showing a mouth of perfectly straight and ivory white teeth.

"She likes pudding," Chrysler muttered out of the side of his mouth to the others, leaning back in his chair, his hands gripping the edge of the table. "Maybe if we offer her some, she'll go away."

"You know I can hear you, right?" the woman asked the mayor.

"Of course you can, I said, of course you can," Bobborn bellowed, too loud for the room, "and I am stunned by your beauty and at a lack of words."

"Really?" Sam growled, also out of the side of his mouth. "This is the woman you decide to flirt with?"

"I think it's cute," Jane interjected, "and won't you join us, Ms…." Jane paused, waiting for the woman to give her name.

"Oh?" The stranger seemed taken aback by the offer.

"Well, how could I refuse?"

The hag, though she appeared a score of years too young to claim that title, grabbed a chair from the table behind her. The man sitting in it stood up and scampered to the other side to take an unclaimed seat.

Pulling the chair to the table, the hag pushed her way between Tiffene and Chrysler. The woman plopped down, arranging her skirt and smiling at the group.

"Helluva Squall," she said by way of introduction, "and I already know who you all are. Mayor Singleton." She nodded at the old man. "Calamity Sam, the fastest gun in the west," she nodded at the red-moustachioed man, then turned to the others, "Plains Jane, hero of the wild west. Tawny Tiffene, socialite and weather witch. And Bobborn Airhorn, gentleman adventurer, and smooth talker extraordinaire."

Tiffene's jaw worked in silence as the others stared, though the sheriff and mayor looked at her with his mouth open. Bobborn smiled, stood, and leaned over to take Helluva's hand. She extended her gnarly appendage, and the big man took it and kissed the back gently.

"I say, I say," he said, standing upright, but not letting go of her fingers, "you've hit the nail on the head! And your powers of perception are as incredible as your beauty. As I live and breathe, I have never met a woman like you!"

"You can say that again," Sam muttered.

"Well, then I shall repeat it. I have never…" Bobborn began.

"Ms. Squall," Jane interrupted, "it's a pleasure to make your acquaintance." The plainswoman took the woman's hand from Bobborn and shook it furiously. "What did you say about witches?" Jane asked, settling back into her seat and ignoring the look from Bobborn.

"Oh, right to business! I like that!" Helluva exclaimed. "They're thirteen women who meet under the light of the full moon. They dance naked under Luna's icy gaze and sacrifice children in their horrific rituals. Or goats. Or a pigeon. They sacrifice things is the point, and they're totally evil!"

The group exchanged glances, their gaze stopping on Chrysler, waiting to take their cues from him.

"Um…" the mayor said, stroking the barrel of the shotgun leaning against the table beside him, "there may be some truth to what she says. We do have a group of women who…"

"I don't think you should just condemn a group of ladies who get together and celebrate being women," Tiffene said, "and to just make them a target is deplorable."

"But another woman was the one that pointed it out," Sam pointed out, "so it's not like we're being sexist or something that like stupidity."

"Look," Jane interjected, "we came here because there was trouble…"

"And because there's a reward," Sam added.

"Yes, that too," Jane continued, nodding at the gunslinger, "but we should investigate every option we're presented with. And I haven't heard of any other options yet. Have any of you?"

The others stared at her, except for Bobborn and Helluva, who stared at one another.

Bobborn licked his lips, watching the woman's face with a small smile. "We could," Bobborn breathed, "go to the fields after dark and see what's what."

All eyes went to the big man. When he saw Helluva's face twist with unreadable emotion, he shook his head and looked around.

"You shouldn't do that," Helluva said. "People go missing that way, end up gone, and never come back."

"But this is Plains Jane," Chrysler said, "and her infamous posse! She jacked up the Jackal of Johannesburg. She trounced the Terrible Trio of Tin Town. She beat down the Barkley Brothers of Bremerton. I don't think this woman can be beat!"

"Well, hold on here," Jane held up her hands, "those

didn't happen quite the way most folks tell them tales."

"I think it's a good idea," Tiffene sniffed. "Let's go out in the dark of night, prowl around the cornfields, which are higher than our heads, and see if we can figure out what's going on. I know I can handle myself, but I'm not so sure about the rest of you."

"Oooh," Sam growled, "now look here, missy, ain't no one gonna sit here and call me a coward or tell me I can't do something!"

"Wait a second, Sam," Jane turned towards the smaller man, "I don't reckon that's exactly what Tiffene was gettin' at."

"No, it wasn't," the dark-skinned woman agreed, and Jane sighed, "but it doesn't mean that Sam isn't not incompetent."

"Yeah!" Sam agreed, brightening and pointing at Tiffene, then stopped and tilted his head. "Just a cotton-picking minute…" Sam started muttering, and ticking off his fingers, repeating what she had said.

"So, it's agreed then!" Bobborn bellowed and turned to Helluva. "Don't you worry, little lady, we'll take care of this, and then I'll come right back here, and we can pick up where we left off!"

## 12. Fielding Questions

"Didn't even think to ask for a map, did ya? Ya dad-burned idjit," Sam grumbled.

"I was too busy wooing the lady fair," Bobborn said, waving away the question, "something I'm sure you wouldn't know anything about, good sir."

"Thinking with his rooster is more like it," Plains Jane said to Tiffene.

The four walked along a dirt track, the town in the distance on one side and a field on the other. The humidity clung to the field, a thick sensation that made anyone passing feel sluggish. The setting sun turned the late summer corn stalks to a waving ocean of green and pale yellow. Topped by the droning whine of the cicadas and the sharp buzz of flying insects, the entire scene seemed designed to make someone sit a spell under a tree and let their minds wander. The problem with settling down and relaxing in a place like this is that it usually meant that no one would ever see you again.

The two women watched the field, ignoring the bickering men a handful of paces ahead of them. Every minute or so, even at a mosey, they passed a humanoid form strung up on a giant wooden 'X'. Each one was set a half-dozen paces into the corn, raised above the verdant crop. A second row of the things sat further back than the first and alternated positions.

They were weathered, but not faded. If anything, the colors appeared more vibrant than the surrounding colors. Each had a hat, but not the standard floppy hat that most folks thought of for a scarecrow. Some had those, but others had leather hats, or short, curved brims, and others even had metal helms like a conquistador would wear when the invaders came over to Northern and Southern Mirron and tried to conquer the dasism there.

The faces of the straw (presumably) stuffed constructs were in shadow, the setting sun behind them. The wind rippled their clothing, making it look like they were twitching in the dying rays of light. Dark gashes cut across the faces where the eyes and mouth should be, and malformed lumps defined the brow, nose, and chin.

Crows scattered up from the fields as the sun touched the horizon and began sinking below. The birds screamed as they rose into the color bands of the harbinger of night, and Tiffene watched them with the interest of a woman who read portents in tea leaves and tossed bones.

"A murder," she breathed.

"Pardon me?" Jane asked. "What was that?"

"It's called a murder of crows; did you know that?" Tiffene turned her brown eyes to the tanned woman. "But not because they precede a murder, rather because they will often congregate after a murder, waiting for the carrion. Crows are surprisingly intelligent, recognizing people, or even places where previous generations had been shot at by some farmer."

"So," Jane asked in hushed tones, "what do you think they're doing here, now, tonight?"

"Getting out of Dodge," Tiffene watched the flock circle above, calling to one another, "but not so far that they can't enjoy the spoils of war."

The sound of the hammer being drawn back clicked

beside Tiffene, and she looked over to see Jane hunched and watching the corn field.

The men—far ahead of them but still within earshot—stopped arguing, and walking, at the sound of the sidearm cocking. They turned to look at the women. Sam drew his pistols, cocking both. Bobborn drew his derringer with one hand and pulled a short Billy club from his jacket with the other.

"What?" Sam whispered back to them, his overly loud word cutting through the call of the crows.

"I-," Bobborn began, but Sam laid a gentle hand on the man's arm, silencing him.

"Something is coming," Tiffene said, her hands rotating around one another.

Small whirls of crystalline frost spun away from her movements as she called upon her innate wizardly abilities.

See, something most folks never realize—largely because it's buried in the past—is that there are five primary magics, then dozens of combinations. Wizardry called upon the ley lines and elemental forces, and the other types had their own areas of specialty. But Tawny Tiffene wasn't the best at what she did. She could reach out and manipulate the water and air ley lines, but no fire or earth. In fact, she repelled those two, while drawing on the others. It was an odd dichotomy, but she'd honed it into a skilled craft that was rarely matched in her specialty.

"What? What's coming?" Jane hissed, reaching out with her free hand to grip Tiffene's shoulder.

Clouds rolled across the sunset, and the colorful bands of nature's fireworks turned blood red across half of the celestial expanse. The wind picked up, and dead leaves crackled and twirled between the legs of the four.

"So, many things," Tiffene said, "and all of them hungry for something they can't get on the other side. They come from the west but were born in the east and south. They tread where no man can walk, but never walk where a man has broken bread in companionship. They're the antithesis of coming together. Instead, they represent all things that creep, crawl, and stalk—"

Jane's hand cracked on the other woman's cheek, and Tiffene's head snapped to one side.

Sam stared at the exchange, wide-eyed. "Ooooooh," the mustachioed man said.

"You were talking mumbo jumbo," Jane explained, looking chagrined.

"No, I wasn't!" Tiffene responded, indignant.

"Yes, you were," Jane huffed. "You'd been prattling on for like five minutes. The sun's almost set. Look for yourself!"

Jane pointed to the west, and Tiffene turned to look towards the last sliver of sunset. The weather-witch froze, words in her throat sticking and coming out as a choked noise. Her shaking hand came up to point. The others—the men coming up beside them, having travelled back down the road—looked in that direction.

The scarecrows were gone from their posts and crosses.

## 13. Popping Corn

Jane watched the plants sway and rustle. The suggestion of movement among the darkening vegetable towers hinted at dark things sliding between stalks and leaves. Something was out there, shifting and stumbling around the ever-darkening twilight, amidst the purple fireflies that lit up among the corn silk and lazily floated upward in rising spirals.

The circling crows' raucous cries intensified; they peeled away and headed west, towards the setting sun. A covey of pheasants burst from somewhere distant in the field, their frightened titter cutting off suddenly by a short, harsh scream. Jane wasn't sure if it was from the birds, or whatever got the birds.

Tendrils of mist uncurled from the field in front of the group, the wisps gathering into ropey arms of fog. The cloying humidity felt like it was flexing in moist showmanship, gathering its strength for some feat of intimidation and domination.

The movement pulled the horsewoman's attention again. Plains Jane couldn't be sure if it was truly the scarecrows. She hadn't seen them move at all, except for the wind tugging at their clothing. But that was before they'd disappeared into the twilight when no one was looking. She squinted into the darkness, trying to discern any threat ahead of her and her friends.

A thick, strong, and calloused hand gripped her shoulder. She spun around and took a step away, putting her a single stride closer to the cornfield. Her left hand, holding her six-shooter, came up in a smooth motion, and her right hand jerked the rifle from the buckskin sleeve across her back. The barrels of both guns leveled at whatever had grabbed her.

She saw Bobborn's shifting eyes over the top of her weapons, the man's gaze fixated on the field behind her.

"Did you see it?" Bobborn whispered, which was still louder than most people spoke in normal conversation.

"There was a half dozen of them," Sam said from beside Bobborn, "but something else was out there, too."

"The ley lines have gone haywire," Tiffene breathed. "They look like a lariat being flicked for someone to jump over, bouncing all over the place."

Bobborn stood still, unflinching from the guns in his face, watching the field past Jane. The cowgirl lowered her weapons and turned to look at where the others' stares were locked.

A dark streak burst from the stalks, darting across the dusty road. Bright red triple trails of blood blossomed across Bobborn's chest. The big man yelped and stumbled backwards, his hands clutching the tatters of his clothing, his eyes wide. Scarlet wetness soaked into the frayed tears of his white shirt and suit jacket.

Jane's pistol twirled and slid into her holster with a satisfying, leathery clunk. In her other hand, the rifle spun as she worked the lever and chambered a round. The butt of the long gun settled against her right shoulder as her left hand came up to cradle the well-polished wood under the barrel. Her head tilted to one side and her cheek caressed the stock of Ol Bonnie.

It had been her Grampa's rifle, and Gramps took care

of that girl. He'd gotten the gun when it first came out, about thirty years ago, right after he'd gotten out of the army. He'd fought to free the rokairn, but even doing right tired a man out. That's what Gramps had always told Jane. But he'd passed down this beauty—which he'd called his Bonnie Lass—when he was getting too shaky to keep using her. He said scattershot was more his speed now, and she was eight years old and needed a good gun that she could rely on. That was twenty years ago.

Since then, most of the parts on Ol Bonnie had been cleaned, repaired, replaced, or upgraded. She wasn't the same gun she'd started out as; she was better. Bonnie and Jane were almost the same age, and it was like being raised with a puppy. You grew up together, supporting one another through the tough times, always there for one another.

Jane turned, taking her time, letting her eye lead and her body follow. As she spun, she went to one knee to give extra stability to any shot she would take. Tracking the blur, she saw more movement beyond the first row of cornstalks.

"Things are about to gat hairy, folks!" Jane barked. "Pucker yer assholes and look alive, as ol' Gramps used to say!"

The crack of Bonnie rent the air, the burst of the muzzle flare lighting the area for a split second. Shadows from a dozen beings danced on the black wall of greenery, though only a few forms were visible. A dark form flew backwards, separating the stalks of corn and disappearing into the inky night.

Rapid fire pops came from Sam, his guns extended as he shot one, then the other—so the kick wouldn't mess up the shot of the other—and an unearthly scream ripped through the night.

He'd hit something.

The air grew chilly, then icy, then frigid. Crystalized swirls of wind danced around Tiffene, her jaw tight and her eyes hard. She raised her hands, and the frozen air moved with her gesture. A wave of arctic wind rolled away from the four, the air crackling and plants drooping, growing heavy with frost.

The things in the dark slowed, becoming visible as paler shades of grey in the dusk.

Jane and Sam pivoted towards the creatures, guns flaring and flashing. The retort of the rifle played a melody to the underlying beat of the staccato firing of pistols, and a lighter pop sound accented it all as Bobborn joined the fray with his derringer.

The tall stalks boiled with activity and movement as the three emptied their weapons into the dark turbulence. Inhuman screeches and alien screams ripped through the night air, causing each of the four to shudder and shake.

The night grew still as the group looked around, smoke rising from gun barrels, and frost from Tiffene's hands.

A ripple of movement down the road caught their attention. The scarecrows further away were now disappearing from their posts in a blur of motion. The rows of corn rippled, showing that the things were moving away from the town.

"Should we follow them?" Sam asked, his voice showing his reluctance.

"No way am I going through a cornfield at night with those things in it to follow them to the women who made them in the first place!" Jane said, and the others looked at her. "They went towards the boarding house where the witches live," Jane explained, "and I'm going back to my room for the night."

# 14. Boarding House Blues

The group left the hotel in the crisp morning air. Well, it wasn't really crisp, because they were in the west, and everything was a bit warm. But the nights were bitter, and they were leaving in the hour after sunrise.

They left their horses and carried any gear they needed on their backs or slung over shoulders. They traveled to the northwest, across scrub land full of tumbleweeds and cacti. Small furry creatures bolted at their approach, and fat-bellied lizards sunned themselves in the rising sun.

The corn fields ended a ways back, far enough that anything inside of them wouldn't be a threat, but close enough to have a constant view of them. Fourteen farmers and their families were missing after the attack of the previous night.

The four had returned to Adam's saloon, and after explaining what they'd seen and done, the townsfolk began slamming windows and shutters, refusing to leave the building. They'd spent the night sitting around the tables listening to the wind and night sounds and jumping at any noise.

Stella had offered to look at and bandage Bobborn's shredded pectorals, mentioning that she'd been a doctor back east before they'd moved out west. Sam declared that the woman had "done a damn fine job," and nodded his approval, slapping the larger man on the shoulder and making him yelp in pain.

Though Helluva Squall was nowhere to be found—much to Bobborn's disappointment—Mayor Sheriff Chrysler Singleton hadn't left the establishment yet when they'd come in. After the lockdown and triage, he (and others) had demanded many retellings of the group's encounter with the scarecrows. No one else had ever lived to tell the tale.

The night had passed slowly, and the crowd had settled down to rooms or floor space to get what little sleep a fear-filled night could offer. Before the sun rose, but after the cock's crow, Bobborn Airhorn announced, "I say, I say, it's time to get licking!"

The group had departed; the townsfolk promising to round up a posse and meet them at the witches' lair.

Tiffene wore a riding skirt, split up the sides to allow freedom of movement, and the woman was annoyed. Which wasn't much different from her normal mood, but it seemed focused and intense today. Jane wore her typical outfit: Bobborn was in his usual white, three-piece suit, and Sam was in the same outfit he always wore of blue dungarees, a red shirt, and yellow neckerchief.

They approached a worn-down boarding house, a three-story affair of wooden slats and a split-rail fence. Peeling blue and yellow paint decorated bent shutters and warped wooden siding. The yard was littered with weeds and wildflowers, competing with rough grass that fought against the arid climate. A vegetable garden beside the house—right next to the well pump—flourished, showing a dozen different herbs, as well as corn, sunflowers, peppers, tomatoes, and other edible plants.

A scraggly dog—more skin and bones than anything—watched them from his place under the veranda. Rocking chairs moved in the wind above the hound, creaking like someone was in them and watching the four approach.

When they got a stones-throw from the house, the front door banged open and a half-dozen women of various ages piled out—mostly in aprons or flannel dressing gowns, wielding rolling pins and garden tools. Angry old ladies were not someone to trifle with.

"We just want to talk," Tiffene held up her hands, stepping forward to take charge. "We don't want any trouble."

More faces appeared in second-story windows, pale and haggard, and the glint of silver and steel accented stylized jewelry and athames. The air grew thick, like the hour before a storm arrives. Wind-tossed tumbleweeds across the yard, once catching on the split-rail fence outlining the front yard. The coarse brush scratched at the wood railing, sounding like a rat trying to chew through a baseboard.

A flash of heat lightning lit the hazy western horizon, and Tiffene realized that there were storms clouds all along the distance.

"Who are you?" one woman called back.

The chosen spokeswoman had red hair, drawn up in a roll on the back of her neck, a flowing blue-green, diaphanous sheer robe over a darker blue moo-moo, her eyes accented by heavy blue eyeshadow, with dark points at the outer edges. She spoke with an accent of arrogance and looked down her nose at Tiffene from the porch.

"I'm Tawny Tiffene," Tawny Tiffene answered, "and we're here to…"

"The Ice Queen?" The woman asked, her hand rising to clutch her bosom.

The other women on the porch whispered between one another, and the faces in the upper windows leaned forward for a better look.

"Ice Queen?" Sam cocked his head to look at Tiffene. "You been getting a reputation, girl?"

Tiffene glared over at him, and the woman spoke

again.

"Didn't you make an ice palace just to keep people away, in the frozen north a few years ago?" the leader of the board house asked. "And then animated ice creatures to protect your fortress of solitude?"

"Um." Tiffene said.

"Impressive, if it's true," Plains Jane muttered.

Bobborn shifted, looking uncomfortable, his face cycling through emotions.

"You should be up here on the porch with us," the woman continued, "not down in the dirt with the lesser people. I mean, you're surrounded by a rokairn half-breed, and a giant half-breed. The only one worth their salt is your bodyguard, the infamous horsewoman, Jane of the Plains."

The woman trailed off, lifting her head to look beyond the small group.

"Oh shit," she said. "The townsfolk are coming, and it looks like they brought the torches and pitchforks. Don't be like that traitor, Squall, and…"

The woman's word was cut off by the crack of gunfire. She cringed at the noise, as did the other woman on the porch.

All eyes were on Bobborn, who stood shaking, his derringer in his hand.

"Keep her name out of your mouth!" Bobborn shouted, spittle flying from his lips.

## 15. The Thunder Rolls

The mob behind them burst into shouts and broke into a run at the sound of the gunshot. The line of dozens of people in flannel, dungarees, and checked dresses surged forward as one, pitchforks bobbing up and down, and torches guttering.

Sam turned to stare at Bobborn. The large man was gaping at his hand, a look of betrayal on his face.

Sam had known the man for a while now and had never known him to be reactionary or prone to knee-jerk reactions. He'd seen the white-suited, red-bowler'd man keep his cool in the face of a hundred charging dasism on horseback. He'd watched the man not break a sweat at the poker table when all five other players drew steel. And he'd never, ever, ever seen the man jump to defend the name of a woman.

Bobborn had come to the defense of a woman, more than once. But it was her literal defense, as in she was in danger. He'd watched the big guy throw a punch, draw his pistol, and trade verbal barbs with countless others over a woman's well-being. But he'd never, ever, ever seen Bobborn shoot a man over a woman.

And apparently, Bobborn was as surprised as Sam.

But the smaller man didn't have time to think about that. There was an angry, well-armed mob coming up behind him. And thirteen potential witches who'd just been fired on in front of him. And all that meant he was about to be crunched between two furious, and potent, forces.

His guns were in his hands before he thought about it, and he spun in a circle to get the lay of the land. "Dadburn, dagnabbit, frickin frackin," he swore, "snargle brusk!"

Sam knew he could single-handedly pick off twelve of the witches with clean shots before needing a reload, but he also knew that Bobborn was acting funny, Tiffene was building a bond with the women, and Jane hadn't pulled her gun yet. He was a hothead but wasn't an idjit.

He continued to turn in circles, first watching the approaching angry villagers, then looking over the thirteen women of the boarding house preparing to take on an army. This was a no-win situation.

He'd had plenty of those. Many of them with his personal nemesis, the gangster known as Bugs. That man was no better than a common yard varmint and was always one step ahead of Sam. The mobster, from the Federation in the east, loved to one-up Sam. The other man had made a game of it too many times, mocking Sam with his eastern accent.

But this was different, and his father would have told him exactly that in no uncertain terms. But his daddy had been a shit wad and wasn't worth listening to.

Sam realized he had been avoiding taking action and decided to be proactive...right after he checked to see what his companions were doing.

Jane seemed as flummoxed as he was, and she was watching Tiffene for her cue. Bobborn was frozen in place, wiggling his fingers around his gun to make sure he was still in control. Tiffene was slumped, and looked like she was in an internal debate of which group to back.

"Oh, fuck it," Sam muttered, making up his mind. "Hey, old maids, get back in the house and take cover. We're gonna make this look good!"

He spun towards the rushing mass of people from Crow Row, and rapid-fired his pistols into the air. Twelve shots rang out, and the couple dozen people skidded to a halt in front of him, kicking up a cloud of dirt.

Coughing, he wiped at his eyes, then glowered at the assembled townsfolk. Glared would have been more along the lines of what he was going for, but with his eyes watering from the dust, and being tear-lined and red-rimmed, he had to take what he could get.

"Ooooh!" Sam ooooh-ed. "Listen up, here! I'm the rootenist, tootenist shootenist gun in these here parts. So, y'all better listen to me before you go making some dunderhead move and getting' yerselves kilted!"

He spun the barrels of his twin pistols with the forearm of the opposite limb and popped the barrels open. Six smoking shells fell from each. With a movement, he pulled two of the new-fangled quick loaders from the bandolier of a belt he wore, slammed them home into the opposite gun, and flicked the barrels back into place.

This all happened in the space of a few seconds, and it suitably impressed the citizenry of Crow Row. Some hooted and hollered, excited by the burst of action. Others looked wary.

"These here women ain't done nothin' worth stringin' them up fer, but…" Sam held up his hands as the mob protested.

A few angry shouts broke out from the back of the assembled townsfolk, and the crowd began jostling one another.

"What are you doing?" Tiffene whispered from the side of her mouth.

"No idea," Sam muttered, "but go with me on this one, and look to Bobborn."

Tiffene turned to check on the southern gentleman and gasped. He was rushing at the house, via a fast waddle.

She moved after him, trying to catch up.

Jane, bewildered, moved behind Sam to support his move.

"But listen up, folks, I said but!" Sam glared at the gathered people, stopping them in their tracks. "These women may be worth taking into protective custody to question about what's been going on!"

The townsfolk roared their agreement and rushed forward. Like a river hitting an island, they streamed around Calamity Sam—known for his public missteps and verbal faux pas—and moved to take the house and the women within, into 'protective custody'.

The women's hands swirled from within the doorway; thunder erupted, and the morning clouds thickened into storm heads. The rolling sound broke the charge into stuttered movement towards them.

Sam stared in horror and chagrin as his plan changed from a clean arrest to a mob mentality of justice.

The thunder rolled across the barren landscape.

# 16. Waiting for a Hero

Thirteen women were incarcerated, lining the half dozen cells of the small country prison. Endora, Winifred, Sarah, Bette, Elfaba, Glenda, Tabitha, Sabrina, Hilda, Zelda, Mary, Samantha, Selina, and Hermione stood or sat watching their jailor as he spoke to Bobborn.

"Why not?" the man in the white suit shrugged.

"We can't just shoot them!" Chrysler Singleton shouted. "It's not moral, legal, or right. They deserve a fair trial. And where are your friends? Shouldn't you be with them instead of telling me my job?"

"I say, I say," Bobborn said, "you've got the problem in the palm of your hands. Why wouldn't you take care of it, nice and easy?"

"Because it ain't right!" Chrysler exclaimed.

Bobborn shook his head, trying to clear the cobwebs.

*Or the Bob webs*, the large man thought.

"But they're the ones who set those scarecrows on the town?" Bobborn pushed, his voice sounding unsure.

"Are you asking me or telling me?" the sheriff, slash mayor, asked. "You don't seem so sure of yourself."

The house had fallen under the press of people from the town, and Bobborn had watched in giddy fascination.

Sam had been shouting for the attack to stop, something the man wasn't prone to do. Why the smaller man had objected was a mystery to Bobborn.

It was obvious the women were hiding something, and it didn't matter what that was. It was enough that they did it. Something inside of the man made that truth clear, even if he didn't agree with a shotgun trial.

He hesitated, swallowing repeatedly, and shaking his head again to clear it.

He drifted into the past in his mind, remembering the one woman that had meant something to him. She'd been wonderful. Full of life, ideas, and inspired to change the world. Matilda wasn't beautiful to everyone. In fact, she was a bit misshapen in her beauty. Much like an impressionistic painting, one which a select few find fascinating, and very few found beautiful.

His mind flashed back to the encounter a few hours ago.


The townsfolk rushed the house, Bobborn leading the way.

The women crowded into the doorways and windows, called upon the power of the elements, and the world around the house answered.

Some of the townspeople had shotguns, and a few had handguns, standard issue in the west where life was untamed and wild. They charged forward with wild abandon.

Bobborn stopped, pulled out a cigar and a match, and lit the latter on the heel of his boot. Puffing on the cigar, the crowd hesitating behind him, the big man pulled three sticks of dynamite from his coat pocket. Laying the tip of the wick of the explosive to the tip of the cigar, it sprung into a sparking life of its own.

He tossed it underhand onto the porch, and it bounced into the doorway.

The women backpedaled; their magical gyrations interrupted.

The explosion wasn't what the crowd had expected. It didn't blow away the whole front porch, but it was still a respectable amount of destruction. The doorway blew into smithereens, and the front porch buckled outward, then collapsed inward.

A second stick followed the first, whirling through the smoke and detritus of the first. The third flew through an open window on the second floor, and three women scattered at its approach.

The two explosions shattered the front of the boarding house and closed off that egress.

The mob swarmed around the building, throwing torches into the debris of the wreckage.

It didn't take more than ten minutes before they dragged the thirteen women out, bound and dejected, to be led to back to Crow Row.

Jane had objected the whole while, screaming at Bobborn and the townsfolk, until Tiffene had pulled her aside.

Calamity Sam sat in the parlor of Adam's Saloon. The locals had celebrated him and the others as heroes, but it left a sour taste in his mouth, causing him to leave the main room. He could hear the discordant chords from the player piano wafting from the other room, along with the cheers and toasts of the gathered people.

They were celebrating the downfall of others, and that rubbed Sam the wrong way. He never liked taking down the wrong person, and this felt wrong.

A hand gripped his shoulder, and he turned his head to see Jane standing over him.

"What happened out there?" Jane asked with a sigh and sat down beside him.

"I don't know," Sam sighed in return, "but it wasn't right."

Jane nodded, and the two lapsed into silence, the celebration from the other room washing over them.

"I enjoy taking down the bad guy, you know?" Sam asked after a few minutes. "But this time, it feels like mob mentality won out. You know, when people push their own idea of who's right or wrong on others? And because so many say it's the right thing, everyone else just joins up and does the thing?"

"Yeah," Jane nodded, "I know what you mean. It reminds me of the time I ran across a group of people who others said were smuggling jewels from the local dasism tribe. But the locals did the unthinkable, killed the three people accused, and attacked the local tribe. It was an unwarranted massacre. People are crap sometimes."

"So, what happened with that?" Sam looked up from his mug of brew.

"Nothing, I guess." Jane shrugged. "The people felt justified, and the smuggling stopped. But I think it's because the actual perpetrators headed east to sell the things. One good thing came of it though: a small child found a home. I think it was unrelated, but people always secretly feel bad after committing an atrocity and look to balance things out."

"You're saying that this whole shit storm may make something good happen, like a kitten being rescued from a tree?" Sam asked.

A scream from the main room interrupted the conversation, and Jane and Sam jumped to their feet.

# 17. That Stinking Feeling

The clatter of chairs and the bark of a pistol followed the scream.

Calamity Sam ran out of the parlor, bursting into the main room with twin six-shooters at the ready. Plains Jane was right behind him, her own iron in her hand. The two skidded to a halt, their spurs curling up ribbons of wood from the floor. They gaped at the scene in front of them.

The entire establishment was in an uproar. Spuds and Bud were hiding under a table near the player piano. The young boy was jeering and shouting insults at anyone within earshot, and the dog was lapping from three different mugs of beer. The man who'd been tending the automated instrument was on top of it now, leaping for the wagon wheel chandelier.

Friend faced off against friend, neighbor against neighbor, and—literally—brother against brother as they solved differences in the most primal way possible: violence. Adam's saloon was in chaos.

Jane was stunned. Something stank. For everyone who'd known each other for years, longtime friends, to be fighting one another, spoke of something greater manipulating the locals, spoke of an outside influence. And her gun wouldn't be the right response, and neither would Sam's.

"It's a bar fight," Jane holstered her weapon and pushed Sam's down, "not a gunfight. Let's quell them with anything except bullets."

Sam smiled, shoved his own firearms into their holsters, and threw himself into the fray. Jane watched the spinning whirlwind that was Sam enter the melee. He punched one man in the groin, turned to give an uppercut to another, and scooped up a chair to face a third.

Jane knew this was a release of tension and worry. So many wanted to do something but didn't know how to turn it on an enemy. But usually, they bickered with a neighbor or friend, not beat them senseless.

The woman stepped to the side of the room, moving along the front wall, and watched the bar fight without joining in.

It wasn't right, she knew, but something had triggered the free-for-all. Bobborn and Tiffene were nowhere to be seen.

"Where did those two get to anyway?" she asked no one in particular, which was all well and good, because nobody was paying her any attention, anyway.

She thought back to earlier that day, remembering seeing Bobborn heading for the Sheriff's, but hadn't seen Tiffene since the battle at the boarding house. When the mob broke into a run, heading for the house, Tiffene had grabbed her arm when Jane was yelling for everyone to stop their attack.

Pulling Jane to the other side of the woodshed, which stood next to the smokehouse, Tiffene had looked terrified.

"I have to go," Tiffene had said to her, eyes darting towards the angry mob, "there's more going on here than meets the eye."

"Something messing with the magic spectrum, or something like that?" Jane asked, her eyes wide.

"No," Tiffene shook her head, "more of a gut feeling.

These women are casters and can handle themselves when alone. When in a coven of thirteen, they could wipe out the whole town on a mood swing. The fact that they aren't doing that now speaks volumes."

"Maybe they are really just sweet ol' ladies, and don't wanna hurt no one?" Jane's reply was more of a hopeful question.

"Maybe," Tiffene shook her head, "but they could still defend themselves. The fact they aren't tells me that someone, or something, is probably interfering with their magic."

"And you?" Jane gripped Tiffene's forearm. "We're close enough that it would affect you as well. Are you feeling someone messing with your magic?"

Tiffene shrugged.

"I think so," Tiffene's face confirmed what she wouldn't, "but ley lines are hard to block, and I can still feel something, like my connection is muted."

Shortly after that conversation, Tiffene had headed in the opposite direction, leaving the townsfolk to their destructive madness, and Jane bewildered.

The horsewoman had no idea where Tiffene had headed, or when she'd see her again. She didn't think Tiffene had abandoned the group, but she'd been missing in action for almost eight hours.

The smell of sulphur drew Jane's attention, and she raised her face to sniff the air. Movement in the window caught her eye, and she turned to see what it was. Stepping towards the cloudy panes, she looked out. A hunched female form darted away from the saloon. A small, bright red flame danced towards the building, following the fuse that was its own private track.

Drawing steel, Jane thrust the barrel of her six-shooter through the middle pane of glass and took aim at the burning wick. Stroking the trigger, she fired off multiple shots, and the fuse split a hand-span in front of the fast-moving tracer. Looking down below the window, the sharpshooter saw three small kegs, the word 'gunpowder' branded into well-aged wood.

She breathed a sigh of relief before realizing the sound of silence pressing on her shoulders from within the bar. An unspoken rule of a bar fight was no firearms, and she'd just broken that sacred covenant.

Turning towards the barroom, she saw all eyes on her. Well, on the smoking barrel of her pistol.

"Wait," she said, raising the muzzle of her iron to the ceiling, "I wasn't shooting at ya'll. There's three barrels of gunpowder outside this window. Someone was tryin' to blow up the place."

The room didn't react the way she hoped. There weren't sighs of relief, and nods of agreement. Instead, the room broke out in pandemonium.

Screams erupted and people ran in all directions, including directly at Jane.

Sam appeared in front of the woman, his fists balled up and held up in front of his split lip and swollen eye.

"Oooh," Sam oooh'd, "I think we need to get the hell out of here."

A wall of humanity surged towards the two, and they exchanged glances. Jane gestured towards the window with her chin, and Sam grinned up at her.

## 18. Stone Cold & Crazy

Jane and Sam crashed through the saloon window; arms folded in front of their faces. Jane hit the wooden planks of the front porch, rolling to her feet. Sam crashed into one of the half dozen rocking chairs, his legs tangling in the arm and back. He fell onto his face, breath puffing from him, and the rocker crashing down atop him.

The small man came up, spluttering and swearing, kicking his feet to free them from the aggressive furniture. He checked over his shoulder and saw the group of angry townsfolk inside splitting into smaller groups. Some fought to get out the broken window, others ran towards other exits to get to him and Jane.

"Jane," Sam said over his shoulder, "what now?"

The woman didn't answer, and he looked at her. She stood ramrod straight, both of her hands held at shoulder height, palms out, and her eyes wide as she stared at the street.

Sam spun in a slow circle, his hands dropping to the butt of his pistols, and faced the dusty road. The sight in front of him made his hands drop to his sides, and his jaw drop to his chest.

Bobborn stood at the head of a mob, a shotgun cradled

in his arms. Behind him was the Sheriff, and two dozen cowpokes, cowboys, cowhands, and a solitary angry cow. Every single one of them, barring the temperamental bovine, had a firearm at the ready.

The townsfolk from inside of the saloon swarmed out the window, the front door, and from around the sides of the building to surround the duo.

Sam's fingers twitched, itching to go for his guns.

"Sam, don't!" Jane hissed.

The click and chunk of dozens of weapons being cocked and loaded filled the air.

"I say, I say," Bobborn said, "I'd listen to the little lady, my small compadre."

"What's this all about, Bobborn?" Sam growled.

"It's what's right, Sam." The big man smiled, sliding his red hat back to block the sun. "We shouldn't have come into a town and decided what needed to be done. All I've done is join the locals."

"You've turned traitor, traitor!" Jane spat.

"Girlie," it was Bobborn's turn to growl, "I'd suggest you shut your yap, before someone shuts it for you."

Jane opened her mouth to reply, and Sam raised his hand to stop her.

"Take 'em down!" Bobborn shouted.

The mob fell on the two. Clubs, butts of firearms, and various other pummeling instruments bringing a heavy blackness to them.


The jail cell coalesced into reality, breaking the dream Sam had been having of a deep, dark, dank mine shaft filled with chittering shadows. Something deep in the inky blackness of the depths called to him, almost singing. He wanted to go further, find the source, and discover…something.

The man shook his head and looked around.

Jane was in the jail cell with him. The woman was face down on a cot, snoring softly and drooling onto the canvas surface. Familiar women filled the surrounding cells.

"You're the witches!" Sam blurted, then pressed a hand to his head as a drumbeat pounded to life with his exclamation.

Endora, the older witch who'd been the spokesperson for her group, glared at him, a gag stopping her from speaking. She nodded and rolled her eyes, trying to convey something to him.

He felt dense because he didn't get the message. He wasn't sure if he'd said something else or missed some other subtle indication. He knew he wasn't the brightest match in the box, but he wasn't a complete idjit.

The woman's head was jerking towards the outside wall, and Sam turned to look at the wooden planks and stone bricks. The prison was sturdier than most of the other buildings in town. Few of the structures had stone, but the burgeoning city council felt that shoring up the sheriff's office was wise. It stopped fires and breakouts, or break-ins.

Endora was jerking her head violently towards the outer wall, and Sam felt it must mean something. His hands weren't bound, and he wasn't gagged, and he looked at the wall. Pushing to his feet, he moved towards the stone and wood wall, pressing his ear against it. He listened. The wall exuded cold, and his ear numbed instantly. Pulling away with a cry of alarm, a bit of flesh tore from his ear, sticking to the wall. It was ice cold, or even more. Odd in the oppressive heat of the west, Sam tried to figure out what it could mean.

Endora and the other witches were grunting multiple syllables and wiggling in some weird gyrations that made Sam think of interpretive dance. He hated art and interpretive dance. It made no sense. It was like ballet, a useless art form with no words, and he couldn't understand any of it. What the hell could a frozen wall in the midst of all this heat mean for him in a jail cell?

Sam's attention turned to the outer room. Fifteen men stood on the other side of the bars, staring in, scatter shotguns held up and pointed at the cells. Blank eyes tracked every movement of the small man, and every gesture of the thirteen witches in the other cells.

A cracking noise made Sam turn away from the statuesque firing squad, and he saw trailers of white spider-webbing along the mortar between the stones and wood, then move to cover the brickwork like lace doilies designed for walls, as opposed to his grandmother's couch.

Jane sat up groggily, rubbing her head, and focused her eyes on him.

His head pivoted from the ice-coated wall to the witches, to the line of gun barrels, and back again. A thought came to him: *I'm about to escape, or I'm about to die.*

"Matilda and Bruce," Sam shouted, throwing himself at Plains Jane on her cot, and knocking her back down to the drool-stained surface.

"Sam!" Jane yelled. "What the dad-burned, cotton-pickin', skunk-stroking tarnation are you doing?"

"Um," Sam muttered uncomfortably, "protecting you from the…"

His next words were drowned out by a thunderous crack and a blinding light, which may have been the wall shattering, or a dozen guns firing, or both.

## 19. Getting Out of Dodge!

The wall exploded, shards of stone and ice pelting everyone inside the prison. The wall didn't fall inward or outward. Instead, it blasted upward as a wall of ice erupted from the ground, tossing the thick bricks into the air.

Sam threw himself across Jane again, knocking her back and his forehead smashing into her nose. Blood blossomed across her tanned features, gushing down her upper lip and streaming across her cheeks.

The plainswoman pushed the smaller man from her, not noticing her bloody nose, and stared at the bars between them and the line of gunmen outside of the cell. A sheet of ice, as thick as the width of her hand, had grown up from the floor, encasing the bars holding them prisoner.

A breeze swirled the dust of the destruction, and the air cleared. Jane blinked as the light of the setting sun flooded the prison, the entire back wall gone. It silhouetted a single figure in the amber light; her dress swirling and flaring around her, flakes of snow dancing around her like she was in her own personal snow globe.

"Tiffene!" Jane shouted.

Well, she tried to shout that, but with her smashed nose it came out sounding more like 'Diffene!'.

"Gather what you can," Tiffene said, gesturing at her friends. "I will free the coven."

Tiffene moved towards the other cells, and Jane realized that the entire back wall had been destroyed, not just the part on her cell. The witches moved towards their rescuer, holding out bound hands, and a white crystalline blade grew in Tiffene's palm.

She slashed down, cutting Endora's bonds, and moved to the next woman in line as the leader of the coven pulled the filthy gag from her mouth.

Jane studied their situation. The missing wall had been replaced with columns of ice, which now held the roof up. The wall of white between them and their captors shuddered, accompanied by the noise of rifles firing. Wide holes appeared in the protective barrier.

"We need to go," Jane said.

"But what about our things?" Sam asked. "I can't leave Matilda and Bruce behind. Those guns are like my babies!"

"We'll have to come back for them later," Tiffene's voice was a command, "right now, it's your guns or all of our lives. And I'm trying to save one now, so we can save the other later."

"I know a place we can hide," Endora gestured to the northwest. "It's some old mines that no one uses."

"Great." Tiffene nodded. "Can any of you use your magic?"

All the women paused, looking to Jane like they were trying to reach out to whatever the source of their powers was. One by one, they each shook their head.

"No problem," Tiffene raised her hands, twirling her wrists above her head. "I'll cover our retreat. You guys get a move on. I'll be right behind you."

"Great," Jane took command, "Sam, you cover our tails, and I'll lead the way as Endora points the direction."

"And what exactly am I supposed to cover us with?" Sam growled. "A stern look and a firm word?"

"Use your imagination!" Jane snapped, breaking into a

jog towards the horizon Endora had indicated.

The sound of the ice wall shattering under continued gunfire made Tiffene turn back to the jail. She waved her hands and stretched them out in front of her, her fingers curling like she was grabbing something, then she jerked her hands back to her. The ice columns supporting the roof collapsed and the top of the building crumbled to the ground, a cloud of dust billowing up and out.

The sound of the door being slammed open came from the other side of the structure, and the shouts of angry men echoed off the canyon of buildings.

Tiffene gestured again, and the ice scattered around melted, and a mist rose into the air, covering the alley and the group in a thick fog. A tunnel of visibility remained in the center, allowing them to continue moving away from the town.

Jane wanted to run, to get away as quick as possible, but she had to keep the pace so the older women could keep up.

"Tiffene," Jane shouted, "a distraction would be powerful helpful right about now. Think you could lend a hand with that?"

"Of course," the weather witch practically purred, "it feels good to let loose."

A dozen white figures grew up from the ground in the mist. Thick, round bodies of snowmen, which then slimmed into more human forms in flowing ice dresses, moving through the fog and towards the approaching men.

The group moved away as excited shouts came from the posse pursuing the portly purveyors of power. Shots rang out, followed by screams of terror.

"I think they met my minions," Tiffene snickered from beside Jane, making the horsewoman jump.

"How'd you get…" Jane trailed off and looked at Tiffene.

The woman was skating on thin ice, crystalline blades of white jutting from the bottom of her boots.

"I'll scout ahead," Tiffene bent into her glide, and launched herself forward.

Jane shook her head and focused on the wall of cornstalks in the distance, glowing in the last rays of the setting sun.

The older women panted, trying to keep pace, lifting their skirts and housecoats from the dusty road. Most of them were red-faced and puffing, though a few appeared to be in fine health. The younger ones lent support to the older ones, helping them keep up.

"Just a little bit further," Jane encouraged, "once we get into the fields, we should be able to get away Scott free!"

"Let's hope so," Sam chuffed from the rear of the gaggle of women, "because we sure aren't going to be able to put up much of a fight with no weapons, and these women not being able to use their magics."

They burst through the first line of corn just as the sun set, the western sky a glowing canvas of azure and indigo.

Passing the first of the poles thats held scarecrows, Jane glanced up, and then halted. The women bumped into one another as they realized they weren't moving forward anymore.

"What's wrong?" Sam asked, stepping up beside her.

"The scarecrows..." Jane pointed up. "They're gone."

## 20. Children of the Corn

"They're magical creatures," Endora said, "and they hunt after dark. Ladies!" The older woman's voice was sharp and decisive. "Form groups," she continued. "Samantha and Tabitha, you're with me. Winifred, Sarah, and Bette, you're group two. Sabrina, Hilda, and Zelda, you're group three. Elfaba and Glenda, stick with Jane and you're group four. Mary, Selina, and Hermione, you're group five. Stay together, ladies, and keep your group in sight of one other so we don't get separated. The full moon will rise soon, and once it does, we should be able to break through the barrier and use our magic!"

"Woah, I said, woah there!" Sam shouted. "What about me? And Tiffene. What about us?" Adding Tiffene sounded like an afterthought.

"You're a man," Endora said with a sneer, looking down her nose at the gunslinger, "and Tiffene ran off on her own. I'm sure she can handle herself after her flashy display back in Crows Row."

"That still didn't answer the first part." Sam practically whined. "What about me?"

"Stick close to me." Jane laid a hand on Sam's shoulder. "I'll protect you."

"With what?" Sam squeaked.

"I'll use a stern look and a firm word," Jane smiled, then moved towards group one.

Sam scurried to join her, glancing nervously into the dark rows of cornstalks.

The air was thick and close, the smell of something rotting drifting around the group. It left a tinny taste in Sam's mouth, and he smacked his lips. Rubbing his sweaty palms on his dungarees, he listened to the night that seemed to close in around him.

He heard something rustle, a quick, predatory movement off to one side. He turned to squint into the darkness and heard it again from a different direction. Then another, and another.

"I think," he whispered, his voice quavering, "they're all around us."

"We only need hold out until the moon rises," Endora said. "Let's keep heading for the mines and hope we stay ahead of these things."

The five groups moved forward in clumps of three, each walking along their own row between swaying stalks of corn, keeping the group next to them in sight. They were only dim shadows at a pace or two to one side, but it comforted them to know the others were there.

A ripple of movement behind Sam made him stop and spin around. A shadow slid with silent speed between the stalks, and the gunslinger followed its path. Turning back to the others to warn them, he found he was alone.

He barreled forward toward the others, cornstalks slapping him in the face. Tripping, he went face down, and came up sputtering with a mouth of moist loam. Pushing to his feet, he spun in a circle, unsure what direction he'd been going.

A shape burst from the field, raking claws across Sam's midsection. Blood welled out of the lines, and the man stumbled backwards, holding his stomach.

"Dadburned varmint!" Sam swore, his head swiveling

to track where his attacker disappeared to.

The night closed around him. The distant song of crickets and the fetid smell of rot was all he could make out.

"If I had Bruce and Matilda, you wouldn't be so bold!" Sam shouted into the darkness.

Claws raked his back, causing him to go up on his toes and a scream to tear from his throat.

"Dagum it!" He swore again. "I ain't gonna make it by standing here like some sort of sitting duck. Or standing duck. Whatever. Oh, great! Now, I'm talking to myself!"

The small man looked around for something, anything, to use as a weapon. His eyes stopped on the 't' of the cross that held a scarecrow during the day.

He made a mad dash for it, the sound of pursuit on his heels. He pumped his legs and arms, running as fast as he could, zigzagging to make himself a harder target. He reached the post and began shimmying upwards. A claw raked his boot, nearly causing him to fall. He pulled himself up higher and grabbed the crossbar, rocking it back and forth to free it.

He looked down, and the first thing he noticed was that the ground was very far away. His vision zoomed as his mind filled in what it would be like to fall from this height. The second thing he noticed were the three hunched, murderous scarecrows circling the base of the post he'd climbed. One looked up at him, its dark, hollow eyes black pits, and its jagged mouth gaping as it grinned.

Sam tore at the piece of wood, trying to free it as it dawned on him that he could see. That meant the moon was rising, and it was a full moon, and that meant that the women should have access to their magic!

The thought was interrupted as the crossbeam came free in his hand, unbalancing him, and he felt his arms windmilling with nothing to grab. One hand held the length of wood, and his legs were wrapped around the upright post, but gravity urged him downward.

He fell.

Slamming to the ground, he landed on something soft, his makeshift weapon driving through something and into the earth. A wriggling form was under him, and clawed hands swung towards him on each side.

He pulled the splintered wood from the loam and stabbed it down into the thing's face. Something popped, the burlap sack of the creature's head expanding for a moment, then it went still.

Sam breathed a sigh of relief, looking around. That's when he saw the other two scarecrows closing on him.

Ripping the thick wood out of the unmoving thing under him, he swung it at the closest monster, connecting with its head. Another pop, and a soft crumpling sensation echoed through the weapon. It reminded him of smashing pumpkins, and he watched the flicker go out of the thing's everlasting gaze.

"Well," Sam muttered, "it's progress, and the beginning is the end is the beginning…"

His words were cut off as the last creature ran towards him, its arms flapping and swaying at its sides.

With a squeak of a shriek, he instinctively brought up his stick, and the monster impaled itself on the shaft, sliding it deep into its body. Its arms flailed, raking down his face to his neck. Metal claws wrapped themselves around his throat and bit into his Adam's apple.

The thing's head exploded.

Looking up over the headless shoulders of the monster as its hand fell limp, he saw his rescuer. Bobborn stood grinning at him, a smoking double-barreled shotgun in his hands.

"I say, I say," Bobborn said, "I couldn't let that thing be what killed you." The big man's white suit practically glowed in the moonlight as he leveled the shotgun at Sam.

## 21. Trust Issues

The second barrel flared when Bobborn pulled the trigger, and Sam threw himself to the ground, covering his head with his hands. He knew it'd be a useless gesture. First of all, because he had an enormous head and tiny hands. Second of all, because a shotgun could tear through a wall, so his hands wouldn't offer much protection.

Something exploded behind the prone gunslinger, and it wasn't any part of his body. Pieces of something plopped to the ground around him. Chunks of another scarecrow fell from the sky, still twitching and reaching for anything near to it.

Calamity Sam rolled away, coming up to his feet, his hands falling to his missing gun belt. He stared at Bobborn Airhorn.

"Bobbo," Sam said, drawing out the nickname, "what's going on? I thought you'd switched sides."

The sound of shouting voices rose from another direction, coming closer, and Bobborn looked towards it.

"Yeah," the big guy sighed, "I say, I shall have some explaining to do. You better take this…"

Bobborn flipped the shotgun around, handing it to the smaller man, stock first. Then he unslung a satchel from his shoulder and tossed it at Sam's feet.

"Brought your guns for you," Bobborn shrugged. "I meant to kill you with them, but just a minute ago, the urge disappeared. Jane's is in there also; you can give it back to her."

Jane burst into the small clearing, Endora, Tabitha, and Samantha following a moment later. The four women stared at Bobborn, who stood with his hands held up in front of him, showing he was unarmed. Then they looked at Sam, who was holding the shotgun and had the open satchel full of firearms at his feet.

"What's going on here, fellas?" Jane drawled.

"He gave himself up," Sam mumbled, "I guess?"

"Let's burn him," Endora said, a small ball of flame appearing between her spread hands.

"Hold your horses there, Endora," Jane held a hand out towards the woman. "He brought us our guns back, and surrendered to you?"

"Sounds like a trick, Mother." Samantha looked at Endora, her nose twitching.

"Or a trap, Grandmother." Tabitha added, swishing her blonde ponytail.

"He may have some intel on the other side, either way." Jane pointed out. "And he's been my friend for years, and only betrayed me for a few hours. I say we take him along and see what he knows."

"You've always been far too trusting, girlie," Bobborn sighed.

"Shut it, big fella," Sam growled. "Keep up that kinda talk, and we'll have to shoot you just on principle."

Sam turned to the three generations of witches, all of whom were ready to have a flash barbeque, with Bobborn as the main course.

"Look," he said, reaching down to pick up his gun belt and strapping it on, "I know I'm just a man, and this big lug over here…" Sam hooked a thumb towards Bobborn, "…turned traitor and had us all thrown into jail, but he's not all bad. He's just annoying, arrogant, loud, obnoxious, and—"

"Okay, Sam!" Jane interrupted. "We get the idea, and I don't think you're helping the situation by going on about him. Let's take him with us."

"Only if he's bound and gagged!" Endora interjected.

"And hobbled," Samantha added.

"And we tie his thumbs together," Tabitha said, and everyone looked at the young witch. She shrugged and asked, "What? We can ask his safe word first if you want, but he won't be able to use it with the ball gag in his mouth."

"Ball gag?" Jane asked. "Where are you going to get one of those?"

Each woman pulled out a bright red rubber ball with a leather strap attached and held it up.


An hour later, everyone had gathered at the mine. They'd traveled up a winding path, up to a boarded-up rectangle of darkness. The air smelled of cactus flowers and in the distance a coyote sang the song of its people. The full moon was well above the horizon and cast a silvery light across the area.

The further they got from the town, the more the coven's powers returned. Their boarding house was on the opposite side of town from the mine, and they'd begun arguing how their powers had been blocked.

Tiffene walked onto the moonlit plateau, adjusting her skirts after returning from a call of nature.

"I hate that," she muttered, giving a little shiver.

She stopped to look at the group of fourteen women and two men. No one had removed the planks of wood from the entrance to the shafts, instead they stood in groups bickering.

Reaching out with her own powers, she saturated the wood with moisture pulled from the surrounding air, then froze it. The planks gave a loud crack, then exploded into splinters. The shards of wood rained down across the area, and the women threw up their hands to cover their heads and faces.

"Rude," one woman mumbled, smacking her lips together, "she pulled so much water from around here, it made my mouth go dry."

"Perhaps if the thirteen of you had been doing the work needing to be done, instead of arguing like hens, I wouldn't have had to do that." Tiffene snapped. "Are you all so coddled and entitled that you can't even use your abilities to help yourselves to create shelter?"

Tiffene stared at the group, making eye contact with each of them, her hands on her hips, and an imperious look on her face showed her disdain.

A few women gasped at her insolence, but Endora held up a hand to stall the complaints.

"Sisters," Endora said, drawing out the word with her haughty accent, "our new sister has the right of it. We should have seen to our present need, rather than discuss how to kill the traitor."

"You hadn't even got to that," Tiffene stepped towards the leader of the coven, and jabbed a finger at the woman's breastbone. "You and you flock of honking geese were still arguing over how someone blocked your powers, and where the source was located." Endora opened her mouth to reply, her face flushed and angry. Tiffene held up a hand. "No," Tiffene went on, "don't you interrupt when I'm the only one trying to figure out what's going on. We need to know who's behind this, not dicker of details."

"Oh, that's easy," Bobborn said, stretching his jaw after Sam removed the ball gag, "it's Helluva Squall."

## 22. Storm Front

"Impossible!" Endora scoffed. "That woman has no power. She's a rag picker on the best of days, not some witch who can usurp our abilities!"

"You'd think that," Bobborn smiled, "but she made me fall in love with her just by touching my hand. And who do you think manipulated the whole town into accusing you of being the mastermind of the scarecrows? Then there's the whole thing where she created the scarecrows using bits of cloth rags that she'd picked, and the rags of humanity, growing stronger with each person she pulled in, until she could start taking in the townsfolk. Migrant workers, drifters, railroad hobos, and then whole families and households. Starting with outlying ranchers and working her way into the town."

"Hold your horses, hoss," Jane interrupted, "how do you know all this?"

"She told me," he shrugged, "while we were cuddling after we—"

"Woah, boy!" Sam interrupted this time. "We don't need any details about that!"

"That's fine," Bobborn nodded, "besides, a gentleman should never kiss and tell. Or do all the things I did and tell. All I will say is, wow! What a woman!" The big man sighed wistfully.

"Let's move on," Tiffene said, her dark skin blushing in the moonlight. "Why is she doing all this? What's her game?"

"Oh, that." Bobborn's sigh sounded tired this time. "It's to get us all here."

"What?" Tiffene said.

"The townsfolk will be along shortly," Bobborn said, stuffing his hands in his pockets and rocking back on his heels. "They'll kill all of you, or you'll kill them. Either way, they'll have a bunch more scarecrows, and can look at the next town. Really, they want to take over everything, making everyone their mindless slaves."

"Who are 'they'?" Sam asked.

"That's a good question," Bobborn shrugged. "Helluva never told me."

"I think a better question would be, why draw us here?" Tiffene mused, mesmerized by the mouth of the mines.

"It's a place of power," Endora said. "We've come up here for rituals before. They shut this mine down because of supernatural encounters with…something from the depths. There's an emanation of power from below, like something very strong is sleeping beneath the tunnels. They said that the things mined from here carried repercussions with them. Sometimes people swore it was cursed, others said blessed."

"What did they dig up here?" Jane asked. "Copper? Gold? Gems?"

"No one seems to remember," Endora said with a shrug.

"It remembers," Tiffene whispered, still staring at the shaft entrance.

"Somebody's coming," Sam grunted, his voice

cracking.

The group turned to look back the way they'd come. In the distance, dozens of torches danced along the road. A few hundred meters in front of the line of firelight was a dark ripple of shadows moving towards them.

"Looks like we have a decision to make," Jane said. "Do we make a last stand here, or try to run?"

"It won't stop them," Tiffene's voice was husky and heavy. "Whatever is going on, the answer is below these mines. It's ancient, and it's hungry. What do any of you know about Helluva Squall? Where'd she come from? Who was she before she came here? How long has she been here?"

"Ask our historian," Winifred—a heavyset woman with dark hair piled on top of her head in a cone—said, pointing at Elfaba.

Everyone turned to look at the thin woman, who, in turn, looked a bit green in the moonlight. Glenda moved up next to Elfaba and took her hand.

"Go ahead, sweetie," Glenda encouraged, "use your gifts, and tell them."

Elfaba nodded, her face a grimace of apprehension. She pulled her hand from her partner's and moved to stand in the mouth of the mine. Placing her hands on either side of the opening, resting them on the wooden supports, she closed her eyes and took a deep breath.

· Moments passed without her saying anything.

Jane opened her mouth, about to say something, but Glenda held up a finger, indicating that she should wait.

Elfaba spoke suddenly, making everyone jump.

"They will get you, my pretties, and all the creatures and people you hold dear," Elfaba's voice was strained and wicked, a squeaky groan of anger and ambition. "The One Who Waits Below calls those with the gifts and has long waited for the right time. It has rested here for millennia, hungering but patient.

"A woman of magic came, riding the sparks of the

steam dragon. A man of smoke and fire, who wielded balls of iron and gunpowder accompanied her. They arrived in a torrent of chaos after looting the belly of the iron beast.

"Seeking to grow their ill-gotten gain, they gathered miners, and brought them here where they jumped the claim of a mad prospector. But the woman of magic was small in the power. With the man who protected her, they looted the earth as they had the train. They consummated their unholy alliance with a torrid tryst in the darkness below, and neither knew who initiated it or why. Helluva was brought forth from their union. But the man protected the mother and the unborn babe fiercely. Once Helluva was born, thirteen years passed before the mines turned on the miners, killing all of them except the young girl."

Elfaba gasped, clutching at her collar.

"The girl stole the breath, life, and power from everyone trapped within the darkness," she continued, looker greener than before, "and she rose from the earth, and went to the town to tell them of the misfortune of the mines. She begged the town to come and help, but they only boarded up the dark place, closing off The One Who Waits Below from the world."

Elfaba stumbled backwards, and Glenda rushed forward to catch her.

"The girl, Helluva," Elfaba was mumbling now, her skin an emerald shade, "she swore to bring the town back. She had the power she took from the others, but couldn't use it directly. So, she influenced people, manipulated them. Even…us. She used us, siphoning off our magics to create the scarecrows. Anyone who traced the magics that made the scarecrows would find us at the end of the trail. It was herbs from our gardens she used to make potions to control others. She is a horrible person and now brings her full power down upon us to finish her foul machinations!"

Elfaba crumpled to the ground, sobbing. Glenda held the woman, pulling her head to her bosom.

## 23. The Mouth of Madness

"Well," Endora pulled her shoulders back and looked around at her coven, "it looks like we have work to do. The scales need balanced. We need to free our people—the people of Crows Row—without hurting them."

"Without hurting them too much," Zelda chimed in, Hilda nodding beside her. "Some causalities are unavoidable."

"Aunt Zelda!" Sabrina admonished.

"Dearie," Hilda said, her matronly voice comforting, "Farmer Mac has it coming for what he did to her at the Fall Festival. He deserves a little comeuppance for his shenanigans."

Sabrina looked up and off to one side, rocking her head back and forth, then nodded slightly.

"It won't stop the thing doing this, even if we stop the mob coming," Tiffene said.

"Then we go down and get it," Jane said, pumping her fist back and forth across her body.

"Go on then," Endora said, "we've got this. Go find the source and break it, so this never happens again."

"I don't expect anyone to come with me," Tawny Tiffene said, her chin lifted and her jaw tight.

"Hell, sister," Plains Jane piped up, "you ain't never alone when I'm around. I got yer back, me and my trusty six shooter!"

"And this shotgun, Jane," Calamity Sam added, passing the double barrel to the woman, "And I'm going with you two. We started it together. We'll finish the dang-blasted thing together!"

"I say, I say," Bobborn Airhorn said, a bit too loudly, "I'd like to go, also, if you'll have me. I figure I got some making up to do for my indiscretions. So, if you think you can trust me, I'll be joining you. I'll even walk up front. You don't even have to give me a gun. I'll just use my truncheon here…"

The big guy pulled the Billy club he always carried from under his suit jacket and slapped it against the opposite hand.

Tiffene looked back and forth between her three traveling companions.

"Predictable, cliché, stereotypical, and obvious," she muttered, looking into the middle distance. "It's like those three are characters in some story, and they're driven to follow it through until the end."

"Did she just look at us?" Wanderly asked, his short legs propped up on the table in front of him.

"I think she did," Croaker laughed.

"I love it when they break the fourth wall," Kitty squealed, laughing. "It gets me every time!"

The regulars of The Traveller's Inn were arranged throughout the current saloon motif, as Cogsley projected the images onto the sheet hanging on the wall. Golem FloorSweeper paused in their narration of what each of the people on the screen said.

"Looks like you were right, Jack," Nomed whispered into Jack's ear.

The proprietor jumped, jerking his head to the demon-spawn who'd appeared beside him.

"When, why, how," Jack sputtered, "did you get here?"

"Yeah," Nomed chuckled, "don't like it when it happens to you, do you?"

"How did you know?" Jack asked, recovering.

"I get around, and have the hearing of a halfling," Nomed smiled.

"I heard that!" Wanderly shouted over his shoulder. "And yes, you do, you monstrosity of a man!"

"When do I get to go out on one of these little missions?" Nomed asked, lowering his voice again.

"You?" Jack turned and looked at the man again. "You want to go out?"

"Of course I do," Nomed smiled again, this time more wolfishly. "Why do you think I hang out here, Jack? For the stale pretzels, sour beer, and fondled peanuts?"

"Forgive me for interrupting," Cogsley said from behind the two, "but the pretzels are not stale if you eat them when I put them out. And the fondled nuts are because Darome can never decide which bowl of nuts he wants to put in his mouth."

"Yeah," Nomed said a bit louder, and much more sarcastically, "that's the reason, Cogsley."

"Hey!" Darome complained. "It's not my fault that I don't like those little red wrappers on my nuts!"

The crowd tittered at the innuendo.

"I'll keep it in mind," Jack said to Nomed, "and put you in when I have a mission that suits your specific skill set."

"And mine!" Wanderly shouted back.

Nomed rolled his eyes.

"Can we just get back to seeing how this turns out?" Jack asked the room.

The regulars quieted and Golem began narrating again.

The four descended into the darkness. The opening passage was dry and dusty, the moonlight reaching into its mouth to light the first few paces. Sam took the lead, using his rokairn vision to see in the almost non-existent light. Thirty paces in, he found an old oil lantern and lit it. The yellow glow of the wick wasn't much light, but it was better than pitch black.

Side passages yawned open in the dim light, looking like hungry maws waiting for some unsuspecting prey to wander in to be devoured. The deeper they went, the more damp the cave became, and the sound of dripping water accompanied the stalagmite and stalactite formations on the ground and hanging from the ceiling, respectively.

The fetid smell of something foul and rotting thickened as they moved further into the warren of stone, and a coppery coating from the tainted air filled their mouths.

"Think they'll make it?" Bobborn asked.

"You mean, will those women subdue an angry mob with torches and guns?" Sam asked.

Bobborn grunted to confirm his question.

"Only if we succeed here," Tiffene answered, her higher pitch voice echoing off the tunnel walls.

"What's that mean?" Jane asked, sounding anxious.

"If we don't win the day," Tiffene said with an annoyed sigh, "then the thing below will just keep throwing people at them. They'll have to kill everyone, which means the thing wins. Or even if they all kill each other, the being below will now have all of them, and their magics."

"So, what you're saying is," Jane hesitated, "we have to win for them to even survive?"

"That is exactly what I'm saying," Tiffene confirmed. "And if we don't, then no matter what else happens, the thing in the dark will move forward with its plans of conquering everyone on the continent, possibly in the entire world."

"No pressure, or anything," Sam muttered.

# 24. Shafts & Holes

"Boggers!" Sam yelled as the tunnel flooded with light.

Crystalline outcroppings glowed with myriad soft colors. Green, yellow, blue, orange, and red emanations filled the mine, lighting it enough for everyone to see, mostly. Murky shadows still shrouded dark crevasses in the floor and ceiling, as well as cracks in the stone walls. The light pulsed, giving the illusion of movement to the four huddled together in the middle of the passage.

"Get off of me!" Tawny Tiffene growled, shrugging the others away from her. "Don't be such ninnies. You're fine. It's just a little…"

The elementalist trailed off.

"Magical lights that turned on very suddenly to make things just a little extra creepy?" Jane suggested.

"Yeah," Tiffene nodded, a little too vigorously, "that. You're fine. We're fine. Everything's fine."

"Are they fine?" Bobborn asked, pointing out dark, bristly forms about an arm's length long hanging from the ceiling.

"I hope they're sleeping," Sam whispered, and his voice echoed off the walls.

The things shivered with each word, as if the sounds

were disturbing their slumber.

"Hold this," Sam said, shoving the lantern into Bobborn's hands, and moving forward to survey their path.

Dozens of craters, deep recesses that pooled shadows like small ponds of darkness, pockmarked the floor ahead of the group. The cavern rumbled, dust drifting down from the ceiling.

"I hope that's not an earthquake," Jane whimpered, her eyes wide, the whites showing.

"I don't think it was," Tiffene said reassuringly. "I think it was whatever is below us, stirring."

"How is that better?" Jane squeaked. "Why would you even say something like that? It's not helpful!" The woman's voice rose in pitch and volume with each sentence, the last coming out practically as a screech of panic.

The things stirred, dozens of long legs unfolding from each one, and clicking to the stone around their forms. They kept uncurling, undulating until each one was longer than the height of a man, and black, spindly legs jutted from each part of the creatures' segmented bodies.

"Hush, woman!" Bobborn advised, gentler than his usual tone, but still louder than most people spoke. "I say, I say, you're rousing the sleeping beasts!"

As he uttered the last word, the things came completely to life, and bulbous heads with crystalline eyes searched the cavern, and pincers under the things' jaws, gaped open. Each one moved in synchronized concert with the others, jerking like some macabre dance of the dark, where nightmares play.

The chamber erupted in movement; the creatures dropping from the ceiling and scampering towards the group. They backpedaled, moving in reverse until they heard more of the creatures behind them. The cavern was alive with spindly legs and snapping jaws.

"This way!" Bobborn boomed and leapt into one of the shadowed depressions into the ground, the illumination of the lantern creating a ring of light that receded with the sound of his voice.

The creatures slid towards the remaining three, making them bunch together at the edge of the hole their friend had disappeared down.

"Follow or face these things?" Sam shouted, though the volume was unnecessary.

"We need to go down below. I can feel it," Tiffene said.

"If we kill the big thing," Sam turned to the elementalist, "will these things still be waiting for us when we come back up?"

"I think they're more of watchdogs for the thingy down below," she replied, "but it'll be easier to beat it if we're not tired and lacking ammunition because we faced these things."

"Then we have our decision," Jane said.

The plainswoman shouldered her shotgun and jumped down the shaft without another word.

"Wahoo!" Sam shouted as he followed, throwing himself over the edge and disappearing into the dark.

"Stop," Tiffene said in the multi-color light, speaking to the creatures.

They stopped.

"I shall return for you," she continued. "If you're here when I return, be prepared to serve a new master, or perish."

She turned and dropped into the opening.

The vertical path shot her downward, the smooth shaft becoming a slide. She skidded along the sides, flipping all the way over as the passage corkscrewed multiple times. Then she was in midair, falling. She landed on something large and soft, and a wuff of breath enveloped her face.

"Get off," a not-so-booming voice groaned.

Tiffene rolled off Bobborn and rose to her feet. They were in an immense chamber, lit by the same glowing, crystalline structures as above, but much more numerous. A long table dominated the room, bowls and platters of multicolored glass filled with steaming piles of something familiar in shape, but not in consistency.

Squinting, Tiffene cocked her head at the buffet of delicacies, her mind not registering what she was looking at. Then the realization dawned on her. The dishes were human body parts, but not corporal and solid. They were ghostly remnants of limbs and dissected bits of chests, hands, legs, and more. It was a smorgasbord of the spirit and soul, and a dozen spectral figures lined each side of the table, bathing it in pale blue lights.

"Are those ghosts?" Jane asked in a whisper.

The beings turned to look towards the source of the sound, and black hollows where eyes should have been glided over the group.

"Stop talking!" Tiffene hissed through clenched teeth, hoping they wouldn't be detected if they didn't make any noise.

"It's too late for that," cackled a voice. "We already know you're here!"

The room flared with a brilliant white light, illuminating every nook and cranny. The four companions shielded their eyes, waiting for them to adjust. When their vision cleared, they gaped at what was in front of them.

At the head of the table was an immense, gelatinous cocoon that throbbed and pulsed in time with the crystals lighting the chamber. On one side of it was a being twice the height of a man, made completely of crystal. On the other side was Helluva Squall, swirling her hands around one another and cackling madly.

That was when the alien insects began pouring from the dozens of holes in the ceiling and raining down on the room.

## 25. The Boss Fight, or Is It?

"By the gods!" Jane exclaimed.

"You hoping we all die quick?" Sam quipped, his twin pistols appearing in his hands.

"Nope," Jane growled, flipping the shotgun open and plugging two shells in the chambers, "I'm hoping we have enough ammo to whup their asses!"

"We won't," Bobborn bellowed, drawing a huge firearm from his waistband, "so y'all best get creative in this here fight!"

"Where'd you get that from?" Sam exclaimed with wide eyes.

"In my pants," Bobborn laughed, "the one place I knew none of you would put your hands."

Tiffene said nothing, her eyes locked on Helluva Squall's.

"You shall all die. I've seen it in the bones of the dead, and the runes scattered across the table," Helluva mocked. "And you shall do so by my hand and command, with immense pain. You've been my pawns and toys in a game that I've designed and played for my whole life!"

"Shut the hell u—" Tiffene froze mid-word.

The others didn't notice as they turned to face down the hordes of specters and extraterrestrial bugs.

Sam spun towards the invaders from above, still flooding through the holes in the ceiling. His hands jerked up and down, balancing the recoil of his firearms, each shot flying true and rupturing the carapace of a many-legged foe.

He slammed one empty pistol back into the holster and flicked out a quick load cartridge from his belt into the air, snapping the barrel of his weapon open with a movement of a finger and a twist of his wrist. He pulled the weapon back and the six new shells slid into the chambers they'd been made for. Another flick of his wrist and the barrel snapped closed, the gun reloaded.

He fired that weapon into the oncoming mass of man-sized insects, his other hand at his belt. Without looking or thinking, Sam popped open the barrel of his second weapon and spun the holster. It turned upside down, ejecting the spent casings, and locked back into place as it returned to its normal position. He slammed another quick-load cartridge into place in the second weapon and drew it to continue firing, returning the first to its holster for the same reloading treatment.

Bugs died by the dozens, in just as many seconds.

Jane watched the ghostly diners rise from the table, and glide towards her and her friends, and wondered how you killed something without a body.

Bobborn let out a whoop of excitement, his trademark battle cry, and jumped onto the table and ran towards the crystal warrior at the other end, kicking bowls and plates as he went. The specters opened their mouths in silent screams, their eyes widening to long, black holes as their meal was disrupted.

Jane observed the scene with interest, an idea coming to her. She set the stock of the shotgun to her shoulder, dropped her foot back a half step, and aimed for the ethereal meal. Squeezing the trigger, a bowl exploded, and the wraiths contorted in a jig of anxious nervousness.

"I got your number now, bitches!" Jane grinned.

She knelt, sighted along the table, and pulled the trigger again. A half dozen glasses, four bowls, and two platters shattered as the scatter shot spread in a widening arc along the tabletop.

The ethereal beings screamed silently again, turning towards the source of their pain.

"The way to a man's heart is through his stomach," Jane was saying as she realized that all the beings were looking towards her. "Oh, shit. I think the jig is up!"

The apparitions rose from their seats and shot towards the woman.

Bobborn launched himself off the end of the table, gun flaring as he fired repeatedly at the crystal warrior standing next to the pulsing blob. The slugs ricocheted off the guardian, and it turned its head up to look at its oncoming attacker.

The guardian raised a hand, like it was in slow motion, and Bobborn's neck landed neatly in the fold of the creature's grip.

Bobborn gagged with the impact, shoved his piece into the monster's mouth, and quick-fired, emptying the remaining rounds directly down the thing's gullet.

The monster didn't even twitch. It took the slugs like a champ. The only sign that it felt anything at all was the slight movement of its throat as it swallowed.

Bobborn attempted to gulp in disbelief, but realized

that he couldn't. In fact, he couldn't even take a breath as the juggernaut slowly crushed his windpipe.

Flipping his legs up, the big man put both feet on the behemoth's chest and pushed. He tore free of the thing's grasp, flipping into a backwards somersault. But instead of landing on his feet, his lower half came down on the table, knocking the little remaining wind from his lungs. His upper body swung underneath, causing his head to slam into the leg of the table, and stars to blossom across his vision.

Flopping to the floor, Bobborn blinked to clear his sight, only to see the monster reaching down for him. This hadn't turned out how he'd pictured it.

Jane whooped, popping open the weapon to reload. Shells ejected, and she pushed two more loads in and snapped the shotgun closed. She still had her six-shooter on her hip but thought that the current weapon was doing the job just fine.

She fired twice more, watching the spirits scream silently as their life force and substance were turned into a fine mist of incorporeal bits. The beings began to fade, dissipating as their sustenance disappeared.

The table shook, and movement at the end made Jane look towards the giant guardian who had stood beside the weird gelatin mold that throbbed with the same rhythm as the pulsing lights. She saw Bobborn gracefully arc into a backflip and bellyflop onto the table. Glancing behind her, she saw Tiffene standing stock still, glaring at Helluva at the other end of the table. The only other one doing okay was Calamity Sam. The small man was cutting down the bug things like a tornado tearing up a crop of wheat.

That's when something as cold as ice gripped her beating heart.

## 26. Live and Let Die

The room melted around Tiffene.

First the edges went soft, and the walls lost their definition, the noises of battle fading from her awareness. Then her friends, the table, and all the other people (except for Helluva and the pulsing sack of whatever-that-was beside her) disappeared.

The old woman cackled, and Tiffene was sure that no one else could hear it or see the woman's maniacal grin. Their eyes locked on one another's, but the idea that she was in a different time and place clouded the elementalist's mind. The missing table cleared the space between her and the witch of Crows Row, and their bodies seemed to draw closer to one another.

"You don't have it," Helluva's voice was in Tiffene's head, "and you can't handle this. I will toy with you while I destroy you. Your little minions shall perish from the master's minions. The short red-headed rokairn shall die at the touch of the poison of the spectral centipedes! Oh, you're surprised by that. Yes, it is true. The 'bugs' you saw are not of this world and walk the astral plane as well as the physical. They will devour his body and digest his soul. The fat man will fall to the protector of the master, and your little pony girl will perish under the grip of the beings from another plane of existence. The master has been here a long time, fought many battles against wizards and warriors in many forms, and came out of each fight with a new weapon against the people of this reality."

"Wait," Tiffene panted in her mind, "I have one question, maybe two. No, three!"

"I will entertain myself as you squirm," Helluva replied. "Ask your questions."

"First," Tiffene said in her head, "do you really think you're scary? Two, do you honestly think that I care about anything you're telling me? Third, did you really not see what's behind you while you did some lame monologue?"

"Wha-?" Helluva's incorporeal form spun to look behind her.

"Amateur," Tiffene muttered, gathering her thoughts and power.

The elementalist knew she couldn't rely on her powers over ice and wind in this mind trap, but she had more than that to her. She was terrified, but she was used to that. She was constantly worried about hurting others with her abilities, which was why she had few associates and fewer friends. But here, now, in this place, she was complete. The woman had drawn her into herself where she was akin to an internal rain of hellfire, or a hurricane that had bred with a blizzard.

Tiffene sought her connection to air and water and found them distant. There wasn't very much of either in this place, but there was something else. As an elementalist, Tiffene had very specific strengths and aptitudes. As a woman and a fighter, she had so much more. The sheer willpower to bend the elements to her will take more than just some connection. It took sheer, raw power.

And she had that, in spades.

Pulling on her will and letting the thin connection to the elements fall away, she called upon the unseen control over her own mind and will and focused it into a single shaft. A spike of her own mind ripped from her astral form and shot forward towards Tiffene's foe. A dozen other spines burst outward from her mental construct.

The shafts shot outward, piercing the bloated sack of protoplasm next to the woman, and the lance of psychic energy tore through the woman's chest. Not into it, but in and beyond.

The imagery of the imagined world ruptured, and reality slid back into place. The slug-like being reared back, its slimy carapace tearing at the movement.

Tiffene watched Helluva dramatically clench her chest, and fall to her knees, then backwards until her head smacked against the stone floor. Looking around the room, she saw Bobborn flop to the ground, roll to his feet, and shake his head to clear it.

Behind her, she saw Jane arched forward, her body in a rictus of pain as a glowing blue specter standing behind her twisted its arm inside of the horsewoman's chest.

The insects swarming Sam stopped their synchronized movements and scattered in a chaotic pattern more true to their species.

Then the room rumbled, and chunks of rock fell from the ceiling to crash to the floor, exploding into small clouds of dust and sand.

Bobborn rose to his feet, shaking his head. The room spun around him, and in the center of his vision was the giant crystal warrior that shrugged off bullets like he was throwing clods of cow dung. But he'd dropped the gun, and his truncheon swung on a leather strap around his wrist.

Reaching behind him, and leaning way back, he grabbed a tall, ladder-back chair in each hand. With a grunt, he swung the two pieces of furniture at the behemoth. The chairs came together, slamming and shattering on the warrior in front of him. Chips of colored glass flew off the monster with the impact.

The quivering mass of a chitinous slug spasmed next to the big man, and he wondered if the boss was being beaten about its non-existent head and shoulders by some unseen force. That thought inspired the big man's next move.

With a jerk of his wrist, and a small jump, Bobborn swung his Billy club into his palm and brought it down on the construct's head. The crystal warrior staggered, stumbling backwards and falling to its knees, its head splitting. Bobborn laid into it, the phantom sounds of a ragtime player piano, plunking out a comical theme song to accompany the thwacks and whacks. Shards flew, and the thing threw up its hands to protect its head.

Bobborn shifted his attacks to the monstrosity's wrist, breaking them off at the joints. With a whoop, he laid into his foe, and went to town.

Plains Jane felt her heart grow icy, then slow and stutter. Turning her head, she looked at the ghostly form behind her who held her life-pumping organ, and her face twisted in rage.

She'd faced bandits, cattle rustlers, and train robbers. She wasn't going to let some half-formed haunt from a kid's story take her down. Besides, Bullseye was back in town, waiting for her to brush him down and give him treats. And no one, not even a death spirit from some penny dreadful, would stop her from getting back to her horse.

Jane threw herself forward, and over the table, and rolled onto the floor on the other side, coming up with her pistol in one hand, and the shotgun planted against her shoulder in the other. She saw the creature looking up at the crystal structures in the ceiling, jutting out like otherworldly chandeliers.

Pivoting the weapons to take aim, she blasted them with both barrels. The thing opened its mouth in a silent scream of horror and pain, showing she'd guessed correctly in what was holding them here.

It faded from existence, as did the remaining wraiths. Then the sky began falling.

## 27. The Sky is Falling

Chunks of stone fell from overhead, smashing to the floor, exploding with loud pops and sending up clouds of dust. The place was coming down around them.

Calamity Sam fired one more time, blasting the last creature to its final rest. The beast flipped into the air, flying backwards and landing upside down, its dozens of legs stroking the air like some horrific piece of art.

Sam turned in a circle to check on the others, a hunk of rock shattering beside him. Plains Jane swooned on her feet, staring up at the ceiling. She stood amidst the fading forms of the ghostly diners, shards of colored crystal tinkling and sparking at her feet. Tawny Tiffene was looking back at him, dazed, her mouth hanging slack. Bobborn hunched over his broken foe, pummeling the wrecked form of the armored warrior. The bulbous thing that Helluva and the guardian were protecting writhed backwards, but looked more like it was in its death throes.

"Come on, kids!" Sam shouted. "The cave is collapsing, and we need to get outta here!"

The others looked at him and then shuffled over to follow his lead.

"Oh!" Sam gasped as he realized what he'd done.

"Great, now I need to be the leader of this motley band? How the hell do we get back up to breathable air without getting crushed?"

He wasn't asking anyone in particular, which was good, because no one answered. They'd slid down a rock tube to get here, and he had no idea how to lead everyone back to the surface and fresh air. And even if he did, the townsfolk might be waiting to kill them all if the witches hadn't done their part. The others milled around him as he looked for a way up.

"Helluva Squall got down here," he muttered, "and I bet she didn't take the express chute, so there must be a way back up."

With decades of experience living underground, he eyed the sheer walls around him. He tracked the fractures made by stress; the ridges made by pressure; and the lines made by the collapse of the chamber. Squinting at a stone anomaly blinking in and out of the colors of the pulsating crystals, Sam took aim with both pistols and fired.

A loud crack came from the rock wall, and the smooth face and part of the ceiling crashed down. Sam jumped, his eyes going to the dim corner where the collapse was settling. An odd indentation in the remaining wall stood out in front of him. A dim stairway leading up, almost hidden, showed the path that Helluva probably used to get down here.

"Everyone, grab the shoulder of the person in front of you and don't get separated," he shouted. "I'll find a way for us to get out!"

Tiffene gripped his shoulder, and he lurched forward. He knew his rokairn vision was their best bet to lead them through the subterranean labyrinth, and he would do it, or they'd all die with him trying.

He ran, dodging the collapsing ceiling, and put his boot on the first step. Moving through the growing darkness as the crystals went dark, his eyes adjusted. Using the remaining dim glow of the remnants of the luminescent rocks, he led the group up to what he hoped was freedom.

Sibilant whispers rasped from side passages, and Sam wondered what else waited in the dark. Checking down one tunnel as he moved past it, he saw dozens of glowing eyes watching him. A low thrumming rose, like a distant drumbeat—if a drum was the size of a wagon.

Sam had never been a leader, and he knew it. He was much more of a lone wolf. Look out for numero uno, and to hell with anyone else. That's why he traveled alone. This thing of looking out for others just wasn't his style. The thought of just leaving them behind, saving himself, came to mind. He considered, just for a moment.

"Naw," he muttered, "I might need them for something. Maybe. Probably."

"What was that?" Tiffene asked, her voice stronger than it had been before.

"Oh, nothing," Sam grumbled. "Just saying how much I like you guys."

The group piled out of the mine, coughing from the dust. They fell to the ground, and a dull boom came from deep within the shafts behind them. A cloud of detritus billowed out of the mouth of the tunnels, and the mouth of the mines crumbled in a mini rockslide, sealing the opening.

Thirteen battle-tired women stared at them. Behind the witches, dozens of townsfolk sat on rocks, or stood around talking in small groups. Pitchforks and rifles leaned against rock outcroppings, and everyone was covered with dust. Dark, charred pits littered the landscape, looking suspiciously like lightning strikes.

"We were just about to give up on you and head back to town," Endora said, one hand on a hip. "Looks like you fared as poorly as we did. Ladies, see what you can do to help them so we can all go home."

The women took charge, much to Sam's visible relief. Taking care of others just wasn't his bag. A dozen hands, including some of the townsfolk, reached out to help the group of heroes to their feet, guiding them further away from the collapsed cave and helped them settle to the ground. The helpers pressed canteens into each of the group's hands, and they drank greedily.

"What happened down there?" Elfaba asked, her skin now a deep emerald green.

"How about we save that for when we have a cool mug of Samuel Adams's brew in our hands?" Sam said, coughing.

They celebrated the four as the saviors of the day, and food and booze flowed freely. None of them wanted to talk about it, but Calamity Sam told a tale of heroism and danger that pleased the crowd in the common room of the saloon. They were treated like royalty, and someone paid for their rooms, others bought their food, and most of the crowd covered rounds of drinks.

When they went to bed, it felt much later than it was, but it had been an eventful day. After a quick bath using the supplied pitcher and bowl, Sam stripped down and collapsed onto the bed, snoring almost before his head hit the pillow.

The next morning, most of the town came out to see them off. A group of women gathered around Bobborn, giggling, and swooning at his every word. Sam didn't have the big man's charisma, but one portly woman in a gingham dress stood to one side, smiling shyly at him from under her lashes. The small man blushed and smiled back at her, giving a little wave.

Jane nuzzled Bullseye's muzzle, stroking his neck and running her fingers through the stallion's mane. Bullseye nickered and snuffled at her hands and satchel, searching for extra treats. She produced a sliced apple and three sugar cubes, feeding them to him one at a time, laughing all the while.

"Tawny Tiffene," said a commanding, matronly voice.

The elementalist turned and saw Endora, the other women of the coven, arrayed behind her, and Mayor-Sheriff Chrysler Singleton standing beside her, holding her hand.

"Yes," Tiffene sighed, "what is it?"

She was sure she knew what it was. Here was a powerful woman, knowledgeable in the ways of magic, who ran this territory. And she was standing here with the most powerful man in town. This was going to be the expected dressing down for being a woman who traveled alone and didn't have…whatever it was, this older woman thought she should have.

"You did well, girl," Endora began, breathing a sigh of relief.

The women behind their leader nodded. Tiffene wondered if the woman was nervous about saying that. The tension seemed to melt from Endora, her shoulders dropping a bit, and her posture relaxing. Chrysler squeezed the woman's hand encouragingly, and Endora glanced at him with a small, and seemingly wistful, smile.

"You did much more than just save this town," Endora went on, raising her chin a bit, "you brought us together. Because you tried to talk, instead of fight, Chrysler—and the good people of Crows Row—have chosen to welcome us into their township as protectors, of a sort."

Chrysler let out a bark of laughter.

"What she means is," Chrysler said, "is the small-minded folk here think being friends with her is better than enemies, especially after they took down an army of scarecrows, and barely hurt any of the locals."

"Well," Endora sighed, "we didn't kill anyone. But they will have respect for us after last night's encounter. But let's not speak of that right now. Let us speak of you. Calamity Sam told us it was you that defeated Helluva Squall, the woman who'd been manipulating this town for decades. You have a lot of promise. You're strong, creative, and driven. Mind you, you have limited talent and ability because you never stay put long enough to learn anything new…"

Chrysler cleared his throat loudly, interrupting Endora.

"What I'm trying to say is…" Endora continued, ignoring Chrysler, "you're always welcome here. We would bring you into our coven, teach you new things, and let you grow."

Tiffene stared at the woman with her mouth working silently.

"We wouldn't start you as an apprentice," Endora said quickly, raising a hand to stop Tiffene from getting upset. "We know you're much, much too old to be an apprentice or acolyte. We'd—"

"I'll think about it," Tiffene interjected, stopping the woman's verbal stumbling, "and thank you for the offer. You never know, I may turn up some cold and snowy night."

"See that, pumpkin?" Chrysler beamed at Endora. "That wasn't so hard, was it?"

The woman scowled at the Sheriff.

The four said their goodbyes, mounted their horses, and headed back to The Traveller's Inn.

## 28. Epilogue

When they arrived, Jack was sitting on the front steps.

"Looks like you won the day," the proprietor said, rising to his feet. "Wrap your reins on the hitching post, and I'll send a boy out to take care of your horses. Come inside, and we can settle up the reward. You've done well and earned everything you've got coming to you."

The four moseyed in like they'd been wandering the wilderness for far too long, Jack following behind. The regulars looked up from their drinks and food, watching the dusty procession.

Wanderly began a slow, rhythmic clap, picking up the pace as they settled at a table. Another person joined in, then another, until the room was all applauding and cheering. The response tapered off, and the four looked around in amazement.

"Really?" Nomed broke the following silence. "A slow clap, Wanderly? How cliché."

"I could not agree more," Cogsley said, gliding to a stop at the table, "but they did face down an extra-dimensional foe who threatened the wellbeing of this Inn, and deserve some sort of gratuitous recognition. And some sweet rolls."

The automaton set a plate of steaming cinnamon rolls on the table, stood up straight, and stared down at the group.

"Does he have a lightbulb as a head?" Sam asked, staring at Cogsley.

"When do we get the reward?" Bobborn asked.

"An extra-dimensional foe?" Tiffene asked.

"Is there bacon?" Jane asked.

The four questions spilled forth at the same time, and Jack laughed.

"Cogsley," Jack said, "please ask the kitchen for bacon, biscuits, flapjacks, fried potatoes, sausage patties, grits, and whatever else they have. I'll foot this as part of the reward."

"Of course, sir," Cogsley drawled and turned away.

Jack grabbed a chair from an empty table and pulled it over, sitting in it backwards and crossing his arms along the back.

"Bobborn," Jack said, "the money is coming. Sam, stick around and I'll answer those questions later. Tiffene, yes, a being from another time and place, with its sights set on The Traveller's Inn. We move around a lot, using magic that most will never understand. And the four of you helped us out. Thank you for that."

Jack paused, letting that information sink in.

"So," Jack continued, "who'll be staying, and who's moving on?"

"I say, I say," Bobborn said, laughing, "stay here? In some tiny podunk place in the middle of nowhere? I don't think so!"

"I might," Tiffene replied as the big man continued laughing, "go and visit the ladies of Crow Row. They might actually be able to teach me something."

"Naw," Jane drawled, "I'll stay today, then ol' Bullseye and me gotta head out on the range. I hear tell of some airship pirates up north and think I might go throw a wrench into their plans."

"Oooh," Sam ooh'd, "I think I might stick around a

bit, but not really sure why other than you answering some questions."

Croaker stared out the window at the full moon, swirling the whiskey in his glass. Golem clumped along behind him, sweeping, as a small, glowing, growling blue dragon flitted along beside the construct. Jack leaned against the kegs behind the bar, idly wiping a glass with a rag. Everyone had gone to bed, except for a few of the late nighters. Darome sat cross-legged on the bar, Durg snoring gently from the floor below.

"What's next, Jack?" Croaker asked without looking at the proprietor.

"I think I need you and Kitty to help me out with something," Jack said. "But I think you knew that already."

Croaker nodded.

"There's something going on back where Silver and Smith hang out, and it's weird. Like, really weird." Jack sighed.

"Is it her again?" Croaker turned towards Jack and drained his drink. The weathered old man set his empty glass down on the bar and tapped it with two fingers. "Can I have another? And make it something with some age, from the late 2000s, since it looks like I'll be going there soon."

Jack pulled out a key and unlocked a cabinet underneath the bar. Pulling out a bottle of Tullamore Dew, he poured two fingers for the old man into a clean glass. Sliding the glass back to his friend, he breathed in.

"Yeah," Jack sighed, "I think it's her. I don't know what she's up to yet, but at least you're mostly in the know, so I can give you a heads up. You'll need a team, though. Any ideas?"

"Kitty, of course," Croaker said without hesitation. "May call in Byron Savage? Do we need a fourth or fifth? Heh, I'd take a fifth."

Jack snickered at the man's reference to alcohol.

"Okay, then," Jack said, "I'll look into it and see who else I can bring in. Not Silver, he's too busy. But maybe I know a few people who can bring something to the team."

The two fell silent, and The Traveller's Inn faded to black.

"Hey," Croaker's voice came from the dark, "who turned out the lights?"

# The Traveller's Inn

# About the Author

Travis I. Sivart writes Fantasy, Steampunk, Cyberpulp, Social DIY, and more. You can find him live streaming the writing and editing of his latest project from his home in Central Virginia, surrounded by too many cats.

You can find Travis on Amazon, Barnes and Noble, Books-A-Million, and other literary retailers.

# The Traveller's Inn